I0572694

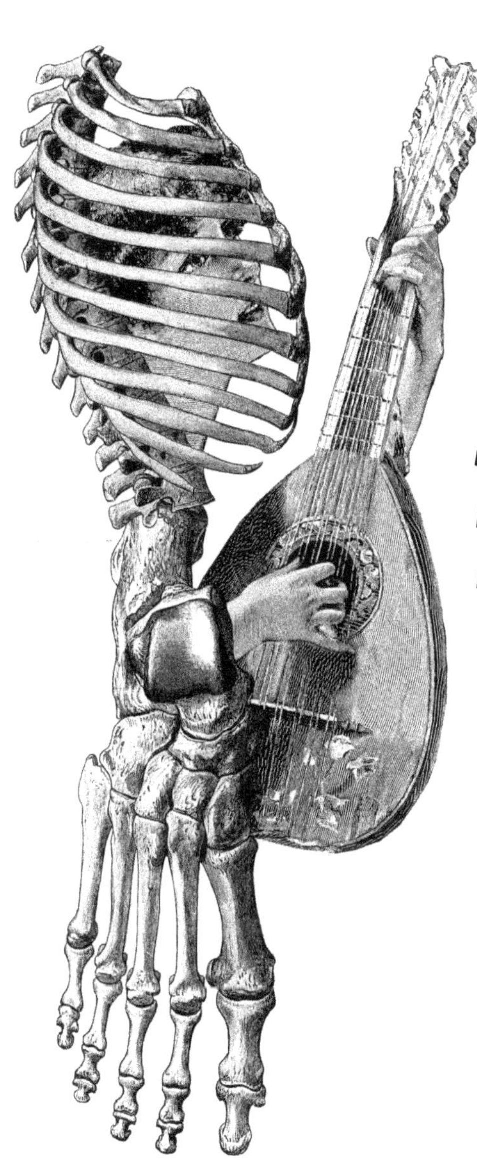

SONGS OF INSOLENCE & EXPEDIENCE

AN ANTHOLOGY OF SHORT WORKS 1992 – 2025

ALISTAIR FRUISH

CONTENTS

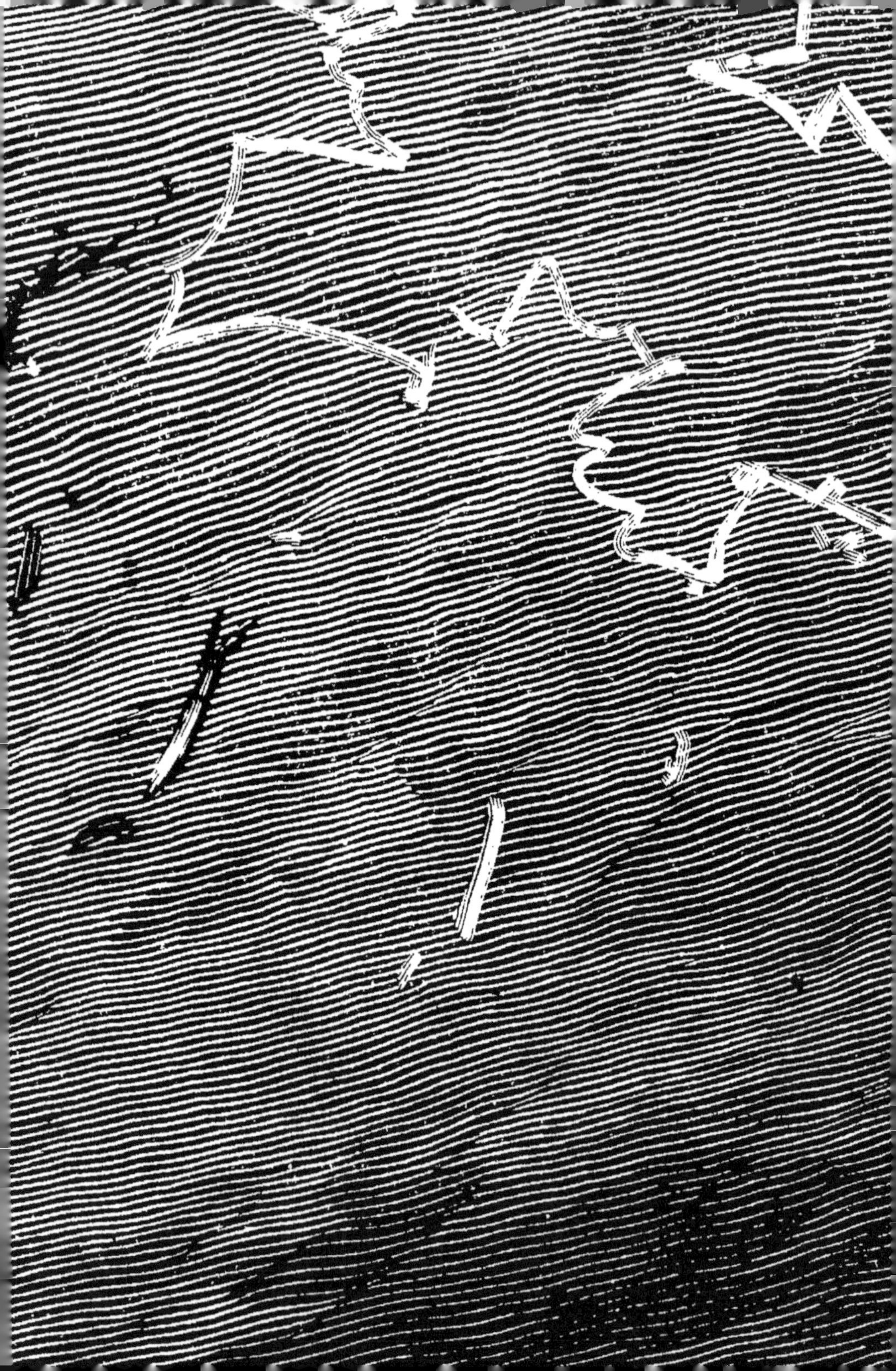

THE ONLY ONES

I have never seen a zombie eat human flesh. They like flesh alright, but they tend to buy it from the meat counter at Tesco, or the butcher's shop. I was the only one who suspected that aliens had staged an invasion. It was in Tesco that I first noticed the clues that led to my deduction.

She appeared to be an old woman, with a bit of a limp, grey curly hair, about five-foot tall, with a weary smile and wearing a raincoat. She was standing in front of me at the checkout when I noticed that she had purchased an abnormal amount of vodka and four bottles of aspirin. Not that this in itself proves the woman was not of this world, it is just an example of the kind of details that I'm programmed to notice. I suppose that you are wondering what a normal amount of vodka is? Three half-litre bottles seemed a bit excessive for a little old lady.

Standing behind her as we waited our turn – the till's

computer interfering with my wiring – I grew more and more certain, until finally I could no longer contain myself. I screamed out loud at the top of my voice that they had landed amongst us and, it was plain to see, they were fearlessly shopping amongst us also. That was when I still thought aliens were bad. But the alien disguised as an old lady was the only one who tried to help when the security guard zombies came up behind me, though I was unsure how they could see me, and attempted to turn me off. They tried to force me out of the store before I could even pay for my victuals. She said she didn't mind if I went in front of her and they should let me pay for my shopping. I was grateful to her and said no more about her interplanetary nature. I thought I should try to find out more about her before turning her in. Though she seemed quite nice, perhaps she was sent here to help us. I was to find out more. This was my program.

I paid for my goods in silence and waited outside the shop until I saw her shuffling along, dragging her shopping trolley behind her. It was one of those PVC affairs that can fold down. I followed her at a safe distance. To be sure she did not see me I put a jumper up over my head. Normally I am invisible. Aliens, though, can see me. The old lady saw me. The sweater over my head made walking difficult, but not impossible, because I could still see quite a bit through the loose-knit wool. And that is how we continued through town. Her in front, pulling her cart; me away behind, hidden inside my jersey.

I don't know why I expected the zombies to care about an alien. The illusion of my emotion almost fooled me, but no one else seemed to be taken in. The zombie on the till at the seven-items-or-under checkout hadn't even blinked when I screamed the revelation that intelligent life existed in the universe; I supposed they supposed they were it. All the other zombies in the queue remained still. Zombie eyes, dead eyes, always avoid mine. Though I too am dead, or rather not alive. Maybe I used to be alive, but I became a robot that thinks it's human sometimes; until I hear the gearing and I remember.

They carried out the operation in the night. They must have done. I remember little about it. I awoke. The world was different. I examined my body closely but they had done a good job on me, I could barely tell that I was no longer a human being. I still needed to eat and shit but I wasn't a person anymore, if indeed I had ever been one. I was a robot. When I came down those stairs I heard the gearing and I knew what had been done in the night. I think my wife knew that I had been picked to undergo this change, or to be copied, and so she made arrangements and moved out a week before I was changed, or made. I cannot blame her for not wanting to live with a robot. Though apparently she knew in advance, I was not consulted and was as surprised as robots can be by the transformation. My reactions are limited by my programming. My wiring hummed and my major valves opened and closed more rapidly than they now tend to.

I awaited instructions but none came. Created and abandoned. My decisions seemed to be exactly that: my decisions but all robots are programmed that way. We are all copies of things. Imperfect copies of imperfect things. I could not locate the person I was based on. Perhaps I have replaced him. I remember his wife had left him – me – but whose memory is this? Whether the instructions are my own, or are created for me, I carry on.

The alien did not move very fast. Nor did I. We made slow progress. The jumper had the added advantage of protecting me from the rain. We reached a block of flats. By the time I entered them she had gone. Perhaps I had lost her to the lift. She could not have seen me through the jumper, so it was unlikely that she had given me the slip.

Aliens wanted us for breeding experiments, so I had read. They wouldn't find me very useful in that department, since the creators had not copied that aspect of the person I was based on. I don't remember the last time I took off my clothes.

I sat down on the floor in what was probably a puddle of piss, took the jumper off my head, picked up a piece of broken glass and tried to open up my wrist. I looked up. She was in front of me. I stopped trying to open up my wrist. My program allowed me to stand up. I followed her to her room. She said that she intended to take me back home. I asked her which planet that was. She made a cup of tea and did not answer. I drank the tea; it may have had chemicals in it. I disengaged. When I awoke, I saw the old lady pouring the vodka down the sink. Alien activity was occasionally puzzling. I was not programmed to understand it. I asked her how long she was going to spend on this planet. She said that she didn't know, and that she had recently altered plans to leave. I asked her if she was going to experiment on me. She said if that meant cook for me, then yes, she certainly would experiment on me. I did not remember the last time I had eaten, or what I had done with the stuff that I had got from Tesco. I told her I was glad she had decided to stay on earth a little longer. I asked her if there were more like her. She said that as far as she knew, she was the only one. I told her there might be two of me.

ANXIETY, BEANS, COW(s)

Don't ask me why. All I know is I have to be there. I see him
coming. It's always him. Although sometimes he's completely
different. But I still know it's him. I've never asked his name. I
try sometimes, but I just can't. It's always the same guy, kind
of. Well, he always has a cow. It happens all over the place,
but it doesn't matter. Always. Every time. Every time without
fail, he has a cow. So that's one way I know it's him, but there
are others. I'm compelled. You see I know I must be there.
Sometimes I put up a struggle, but I never win. I always end up
there, buying his cow off him. I don't know why. I have so many
cows now. Where do I get the money from? Well that's the funny
part, you see he doesn't take money for them. I always offer
to take his cow off his hands for a pocketful of magic beans.
I always say it and he always agrees. I try sometimes to avoid
him, but we come across each other anyway. It's like we are

compelled to meet. It's frightening, but looking after the cows keeps me so busy, and what with keeping all my appointments with him, I don't very often get the chance to think about it. The beans are no problem. I just have them. I don't know if they're magic or not. They turn up by themselves, so there is a strong possibility they are. He seems to think so because he's always eager to take them. I am at my wits' end. I must confront him and see what it's all about. But I can't. Or won't. Or both. I don't know what to do with all the cows. He's not getting a very good deal on all this. Perhaps I could let him have a few back at a reasonable price. Well a man's got to make a little for his trouble. Maybe I could offload them onto someone else. I feel it happening again, I'm going to have to do it again soon. There's no use fighting it, even if I throw the beans away, they'll still be in the pocket by the time he turns up. I've tried before. He's close. I can feel it. I know the routine. No use fighting. So what's another cow? Don't ask me why. All I know is I have to be there.

BANG

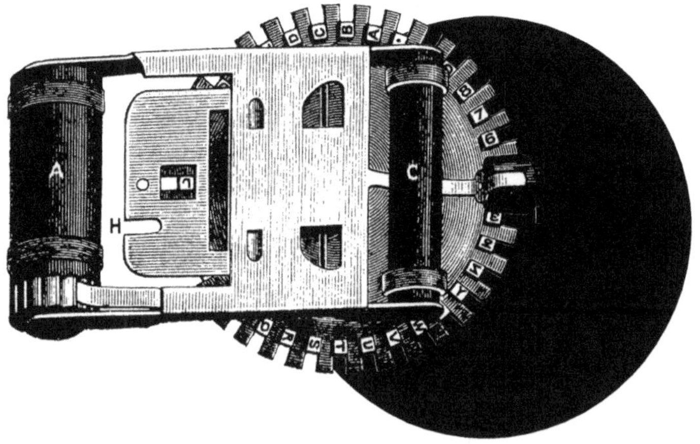

There were no obvious clues to the nature of the shimmering device. No clear way to detach it from the side of Doctor Buckminster's head. Somehow the machine, if that's what it was, began to fire out its message through the agency of the Doctor. Scrawled out over and over by an unwilling hand.

Universe awareness inside each self **awareness each self inside universe** inside universe each self awareness **awareness each universe inside self** **Self awareness inside each universe** each self universe inside awareness **each universe inside awareness self** inside universe self each awareness each awareness universe inside self **inside self universe each awareness** each universe inside self awareness **inside universe each awareness self** **awareness universe inside each self** universe self awareness inside each **universe self inside awareness each** self inside universe each awareness inside universe awareness self each **universe each awareness self inside** each awareness universe self inside **each inside universe awareness self universe each inside awareness self** each awareness self inside universe **self universe each awareness inside** self each inside awareness universe universe inside self awareness each **awareness each inside universe self** each inside universe self awareness **awareness inside each universe self awareness universe self each inside** universe inside awareness each self **awareness inside self each universe** inside each awareness self universe each self inside universe awareness **universe inside each self awareness** inside awareness self universe each **awareness self universe inside each awareness self universe each inside** awareness universe self inside each **each self inside awareness universe** universe awareness each inside self each inside self universe awareness **awareness universe each self inside** universe self inside each awareness **inside self awareness universe each universe awareness each self inside** universe each inside self awareness **inside self each universe awareness** self inside universe awareness each self each inside universe awareness **inside awareness universe each self** each inside awareness universe self **awareness universe inside self each inside universe self awareness each** inside each self universe awareness **inside self universe awareness each** universe self each inside awareness inside self awareness each universe **self universe awareness each inside** inside each universe self awareness **inside each universe awareness self universe each self awareness inside** each self universe awareness inside **awareness inside each self universe** self each universe awareness inside self universe inside awareness each **inside awareness each universe self** awareness self each universe inside **self awareness inside universe each inside each awareness universe self** universe awareness self inside each **universe awareness inside self each** universe inside each awareness self. each universe self awareness inside **each self awareness inside universe** each universe awareness self inside **each inside awareness self universe awareness each universe self inside** awareness self inside universe each

self awareness universe each inside each awareness self universe inside

universe each self inside awareness **inside awareness self each universe**

each awareness inside universe self **inside each self awareness universe**

each self awareness universe inside self universe inside each awareness

inside awareness each self universe inside awareness universe each self

universe awareness self each inside **each universe awareness inside self**

awareness inside self universe each **self each awareness universe inside**

inside self each awareness universe awareness inside universe self each

Self universe each inside awareness self awareness each universe inside

universe inside awareness self each **self awareness each inside universe**

universe inside self each awareness **awareness each self universe inside**

awareness self each inside universe awareness each inside self universe

awareness self inside each universe each awareness inside self universe

self universe awareness inside each **self each universe inside awareness**

universe self awareness each inside **universe each awareness inside self**

inside universe awareness each self each universe self inside awareness

self inside awareness universe each self each awareness inside universe

awareness inside universe each self **self inside each awareness universe**

self inside each universe awareness **awareness universe each inside self**

universe self each awareness inside self inside awareness each universe

each inside self awareness universe self awareness universe inside each.

Attempts to prevent the writing agonise Doctor Buckminster. We are into the third week of relentless scribbled permutations and having to feed the Doctor through a tube. The device's manufacturer, deep nature, and any way to remove it or turn it off, elude us.

METTLE

The Alchemist transmuted base metals into gold. When I met him, I had just started to figure out how to transform *bass* into a few reasonable nuggets, once I'd combined it with a four-to-the-floor. Those long times of just having a fiver and bits of shrapnel in my pocket had begun to sort of turn around. Dosh had started to roll anyway, and I got my mitts on more moolah than I was used to, regular too. Though not exactly coining it. And women were starting to be about a bit, though they didn't stay long. That was when Ra sidled into my life.

First thing he said was, "Safe." Being anything but.

I responded with "Easy." Which in retrospect I was.

And Natasha, my then current, said, "Alright." Which clearly, she wasn't. She had a bigger head even than me, always looking to steal my thunder. Jacked me in two days later. I was a lightning conductor for women who wanted a quick bang and nothing more.

Ra told me that it was short for Raymond, nothing to do with the sun god. Once we started working together, I used to refer to the big guy as *The Alchemist.* The night we met he used his truck to help jump-start the van when I got a flat battery after a gig. We had a sniff or three together that turned into a bit of a session.

I thought he looked like a cross between a biker and a dread. He liked his black clothing and heavy boots, was at least forty-five, more than twenty years older than me and nearly half a metre taller. Tattoos all over his muscles, and locks you could hang yourself with. "Ra!" was defo what you'd be likely to squeal if you ran up against him out on an unlit road. Loads of lamps were out down our way, since the council turned off half the streetlights to save on spondulicks. I relished the darkness. Northampton looked better cloaked in it. Anyway, the half-arsed blackout of the town helped me and Ra with our work. Got away with quite a lot because of it, yeah, man.

Ra was always about after that night, with a bag for his new pal Danny. He liked the *"choons"*. He said they were, "the dog's bollocks". I had a little too much success, a bit quickly, started coming on like I was the golden child. *Destiny Daniel.* I was busy hyping myself into some kind of fame frenzy. My fast-forward future fantasy. The most boast. Nothing could derail the D-train, I was *Dan the Man.* So I reckoned.

I normally grafted on my own. Hired people in when I needed 'em. I was a one-man operation. Never had a partner for long. I was probably a bit much, full-of-myself and a hyperactive workaholic powerhouse on top of that. An insomniac dynamo, always fidgeting to get going on the next thing. Didn't really hang with music people, I preferred to venture solo. If people let you down, you don't pay 'em. Rocking on your own doesn't hurt. It helps to build up a bit of mystery. I'd undermined my exclusive-mix inscrutable persona idea by jawing with punters at venues anyway, especially if they were fit and I'd had some class A. I wasn't exactly full-on mysterious. The sweat of all the graft I put into my schemes had projected up my name and made it glow, but only in the vicinity of Northampton and the nearby towns, or "tains" as the older locals would say down in *Jimmy's End* where I lived, in the shadow of the former lift-tower. I would still hear older people talking like that around my area, but it was fading away. To me it was only marginally more understandable than the Polish and Russian I heard all of the time round here. What you sound like says so much about you. Your own tune. But who knows what to sound like anymore? When you shuffle your location you can change. When you stay in the same place you can alter too. I'd moved around a lot. I was dizzy. In Northampton, I managed to plant my feet, started to feel steady, less twisted. Younger people here sounded more like my old spars up in the Smoke. Sometimes hearing 'em made me yearn for a place that no longer felt like home.

Several hundred people would turn out to my events regular. The rooms would be ram. I'd be quids in. It wasn't like I'd done a big tune or anything. Not like I was actually anyone most people had ever heard of, but then I didn't see it that way. I was already a megastar. International renown. I was almost glad my parents had marooned me here a decade ago. The marching powder made my balloon-head maximise. Soundcloud, Facebook, YouTube and all the rest of the net-chat I got into about my pursuits poured over-proof spirits onto my hot ego, which flamed on up Human Torch stylee.

The Universe – as it does – doused my dreams in a salty, yellow fluid. Ended-up getting pulled deep into the quicksand of foolishness and purest green folly. Though I can't cuss off Ra, or blame the cocaine for all of it. I'd dropped out of college, where I'd almost finished my HND in Electrical Engineering, before I'd even met the bloke.

Most of the money I'd made from the sound system and the wheels in the first six months of my operations I "invested" in *an amount* of powder. Seemed like a major idea at the time. Ra suggested it and arranged the introductions. I didn't even think to pay off my sister who had lent me the money to get my thing cooking in the first place. She chucked me the funds like someone who's paying a busker to shut up, not out of an appreciation for the beats they were creating. My parents weren't happy that I'd blown their investment in me – by fucking-off my second go at college – and so I had to scrounge funds from her. My family all had more than enough cash, but they were always too busy wheeling and dealing with their own shit. All my life they've paid me to go away.

Business skills were strong in the family. I'd managed to make a good fist with the PA rentals, as well as with my tunes, combined with a bit of promoting. But I wasn't cut out to be a shotta. Guess Ra knew that from the beginning. One snort and I would just start chatting on and on. and then give all the coke away to my "mates" – who began to multiply in number. Tooting up a line never failed to put me in a full-on party mood and everyone *had to* join in with my mota-mouthed jamboree. So right from the off I violated rule number one; never get mash on your own stash. I wasn't so hot at being a dealer. What I was good at, I found I absolutely had the knack for shoving the shit up my nose again and again.Till it all ran out. I couldn't make money fast enough to keep up.

Eventually I found myself on a freezing winter's day in Salcey Forest with some connected gentlemen explaining where they were going to plant me if I wasn't considerate enough to cough up what I owed 'em by the following day. I don't know how they planned to dig the frozen ground – they didn't elaborate. They showed me the heat then smashed me cold in the face with it.

"Ya bare fuckin' wasteman, Dan! Ya deep. Wanna get deeper, do ya?"

And with that they left me there all bloody in the icy leafless trees and drove off towards the motorway. I had to hike the ten miles back to town. Ra offered me a way out. The Alchemist was always full of ideas. He'd helpfully bought my business off me the week before. Scrapped the van and sold the bins and decks on within a day.

His solution to my problems was that I would put my unlicensed electrical skills to work for him. He'd fix the debt. He needed help with busting into the railways, to grab what he could.

When he wasn't stealing outright he was kind of an asset stripper. Take what's working and snap it up, so it doesn't work anymore, and then sell the parts profitably for scrap. His main activities involved breaking and burning shit to get the metal out of it, sell it all and move on, without being detected. He'd have lead, tin, nickel, also copper, ally and brass. What he called *"chat"*. which was anything non-ferrous. He'd have it all if he could get it and weigh it in. He was knowledgeable about value. For one of our one-off projects, we hijacked an HGV full of dead computers that were on their way to be recycled. He reckoned there was more gold on board that juggernaut, in the scrap circuits, than in an equal amount of mined ore. If there was metal around he'd go about getting it. Memorials from the crematorium, or stuff from off the top of the church. He'd not fuss. We'd drive about and see what we could find. He said that he "put the coin in coincidence." He saw himself as a kind of miner. A transformer. He could see the potential in an urban component to mint himself plenty of beer tokens. This he released through selling the booty on to one of his network of dodgy connections, which had been massively expanded by the time he'd spent in prison.

He said he'd been *on the out f*or well over a decade and that *his game* hadn't been metal before. "Every sentence, or decade, get yourself a new wrinkle. Keeps interest. Less likely to occur to the constabulary to put your face on the shenanigans. If I was younger I'd get right into computer hacking. There's scope in that, bruv. I suppose I could work with someone else, who's good with them, but I'd never know if they were screwing me."

He gave me that double-bluff smile and added, "Organ harvesting sounds promising."

I never did realise he wasn't actually my mate. During those months that we were together he kept me busy. And when I wasn't active I was snorting up another debt. My direct involvement with music disappeared, but I still listened to it all the time. Ra was into sounds too, but his schedule was too hectic for me to get it together to do my thing. We zipped around the country.

A lot of the graft was railway work. Scoping out took the time. We were very careful. Then the getting down to it, which we attempted to be quick about. I handled the techy stuff, tried to avoid obvious hazards, and did relatively safe isolation procedures, shit like that. And went up on the roofs. That was bare fun. For both you needed a touch of steel and cast-iron guts. Ra mainly did the wheels, the ladders, the loading and the transformation side of things. I was height-happy, I loved the climbing part of it.

Whatever the job, our main method was to look like we had a right to be there. Bold. High-vis jackets; safety-hats; false numbers. Both of our chief targets gave me a right buzz. Adrenaline is almost as good as coke. Lucky for me I had some idea what I was doing. Never got that final killing jolt from any of the wires I cut – though sometimes it was a close thing. I liked doing roofs the best. From up high people look like they really are, small and insignificant.

I was the mineral he wanted from the start. Sure Ra had decided that he would take everything off me first, in order to get me where he wanted me – working with him. He needed someone of the right calibre with a brain for electrics and wires; who was fit enough to climb; plausible looking, and organised. I fit the bill. I know lack of sleep and powder makes some people long term paranoid, but he definitely planned it all.

My criminal career began with Ra. I hadn't done anything much before to bring me to the attention of Old Bill. And I took to it with the level of diligence and obsessiveness that I put into running my sound system.

Even though he effectively stopped my career, Ra seemed to like what I did.

"Dan knows how to do a proper knees-up." I heard him say stuff like that regular.

Once he got me working seriously for him, we didn't have time for any of that anymore.

I really wanted to be successful at everything, even nicking. So I gradually started suggesting harder and trickier targets. If you buzz at the same level too long, it's no longer a thrill. I sort of swept Ra along with me. He was loving it. It wasn't just the cash or the C. He was getting into the rush. We egged each other on. He was trying not to feel old. He was trying not to feel mortal. He managed it for a while, too. We were getting away with stuff that I couldn't believe we'd pulled. I hunted the papers and the internet for "reviews" of our work. Reports of crimes are surprisingly few and far between. Journos are lazy. I had the same kind of passion I had for the music, but in reverse. I knew I had to remain obscure. I didn't talk to anyone about our gigs, and that was a hard thing to do with a head full of Charlie. I wanted *the work* to grab attention. The only time Ra and me nearly broke up our partnership was when I said I wanted to start leaving "calling cards". He said I was "a fucking muppet", and that it would "force the fucking pigs to fucking bust our fucking arses in fucking seconds."

That was the day he went to the doctors. He never told me at the time that he'd been. I figured it out later from the paperwork I came across at his lock-up. He didn't go for the calling cards, but after that we did start to up the ante. Play for bigger stakes.

I learnt quite a few new skills working with Ra. Like how to use the cutting torch. It had two scuba-sized gas cylinders which I wore on my back in a harness. Looked like a jet-pack. One was full of oxygen and the other of fuel. I could cut through the world's bullshit with that bit of kit. One of the things you need to do if you want to go and do any mischief these days is leave your mobile at your gates. You get me? It puts you at the scene of the badman antics. It lets the Filth know exactly where you are all the time. At the very least it can be a "joint enterprise" charge. It was one of our rules. No phones. Could be a bit of a problem… meant that I couldn't get an ambulance in time. Not that if I had done, it would have saved him.

I was up on a church roof out in Northamptonshire somewhere, harvesting some lead. For a change, Ra was up there with me. He pulled a plastic bag out of his coat pocket. It looked like it had a load of phlegm in the bottom. He asked me, "Ever sniffed glue… or petrol?"

"No… No, that's madness."

"Yeah, it is madness. The hallucinations are like nothing else. I want to do it one more time."

He waved the bag at me.

"I'm not doing that. It's nasty. And up here? You're crazy!"

"Says the coke fiend. Man, you're a drug snob." He looked at the bag, "If you had some real mettle, you'd huff with me now, bruv. This is *exactly* the right place to do it. Can see for frigging miles."

"No way."

"I didn't think so."

Ra leant against the sandstone base that supported the spire of the church, pulled out a joint that he'd already rolled and handed it to me with a lighter. "Well you can puff instead of huff," he said as he put the bag to his nose and face, started breathing in the vapour of adhesive. After a couple of minutes he pulled the bag away. "I started doing this when I was fostered, after I got out of the school for the maladjusted. It was a punk thing. Haven't done it for thirty years. Couple of my borstal connections died doing it. But that's not why I stopped."

"You were a punk?" I lit the spliff and took a big drag. Wasn't really into smoking either, but it seemed like the best of the two options. My head started to spin with the nicotine rush. I leant back against the church tower and clutched at the roof with my free hand, overpowered by the smell of green.

"Yeah man. What's the matter, don't I fit your profile? Never hear of Poly Styrene or the Bad Brains... D H Peligro?"

"Who?"

"*Too Drunk to Fuck* is raw. Still my favourite DK's song. Saw him play the drums on it live in Brixton in the eighties..." He put the bag back to his face for a few seconds.

"I'll take your word for it, punk has never been my thing."

"It shows. You want to be something that you already are. Other people don't make that shit real. You make it real yourself. You're from some kind of poncey background and you come on half like you're Mista Grime, half like you're a toff. You should go for it fully, bruv."

"My background is parents who didn't give a shit."

"Well you got parents anyway. They don't give a shit, but let you live in a house for neesh."

Ra put serious attention to the bag for a few minutes, then stood up and wobbled precariously along the precipice of the roof. My heart was suddenly very loud. I thought he was going to fling himself down when he said, "On the other side man, maybe."

I told him to stop fucking about. He said, "Topping yourself is the first right man. If others force you to live, you belong to them, okay, not to yourself. Listen man, to be free takes spirit. It takes mettle."

"Shut up! You're chatting shit! That's bollocks, man! Carrying on in spite of all the bullshit, *that's* what takes backbone. Living life man, that's where you need to be bold. Especially how we live it, man. Now fucking sit down!"

He continued standing, wobbling like some kind of wonky vicar doing a sermon from up on the church roof.

"I don't run from Danger, bruv. But there are ways of putting off the inevitable that I won't tolerate for no-one. Yeah man, suffering long term misery isn't my kind of heroism."

He put the bag to his nose again. I thought I'd better change my tactics. "Hey listen, I've got a game for you Ra, yeah?"

Instinctively I knew that he'd go for it. It involved butchering sacred cows.

"What are your favourite three films? I'm going to take 'em and turn 'em into epic porn blockbusters, man. So, come on, what are they?"

He seemed to think about it for a moment. Sat down again. Put the glue to one side. "*The Usual Suspects* is a bloody classic."

I paused a little and said, "I'd transform that into, *Unusual Muff Sex.*" He half chuckled a bit, and I demanded, "Next?"

"*Seven.*"

"That's easy, I turn that into *Shaven*. Next?"

He looked up into the reddening sky for some time before saying, "*Apocalypse Now!*"

I thought about it for a few minutes, took the last few tokes on the spliff and then it came to me, "*A Cock in Lips Now!*"

I thought he was going to laugh so much he'd roll off and hit the deck. He seemed in more danger than when he was standing up – maybe my plan had backfired. Eventually he settled down again. Returned his attention to the glue, was at it for a good five, steadily breathing in and out. I finished blazing. Eventually the fumes from the weed and the glue got to me and Ra at about the same time. I just remember my head whirling full-on, then leaning my neck over to puke off the roof and it started him off too. Seemed like we were up there spewing together for ages. When we'd finished chucking-up, clutching onto the stone for dear life, the idea struck me that it would be amazing if we could get away with filching a church bell. Ra was becoming more aware of my need to push it further, but I'd just failed his glue sniff-test so it seemed. And he was off his head at that point. Nevertheless he didn't rule it out, just laughed. And laughed and laughed again, till he cried.

He slurred, "Until Sharon died, I tried. I really tried. I had three years of being proper. I was even good. Nice. But since then, FUCK EVERYONE. Fuck you! Fuck… *Everyone*." His words ran together, "Ididn'twanttofeelanything… Ididn'tfeelanything… Thisglueisfuckinguseless… I didn't want to feel. That's going to be what I get and get… and get and fucking get. Fuck it."

I didn't know what to say, kept it buttoned and eventually his words slurred into silence. Once my head stopped spinning down its own plughole, I wiped the vomit from my face – looked out across the vivid Northamptonshire landscape. It looked like the bastard *Shire* or something. Hobbitville. It wasn't even the drugs. That's what it looked like. We started the climb down. Heart was beating fast. Edgy ideas came quick to my head. Sweat all over. Clammy hands. Tried not to think about falling and falling and falling. I paused to help Ra, who despite being wasted on glue still managed to get down with impressive ease.

The next day we did our first sculpture. It was worth less

than a grand in scrap and more than a thousand times that as a work of art. That did make the news. Police were looking for art thieves. We were not your normal art thieves. We fragged it with my *jetpack*. Not only had we destroyed a famous work, by someone dead who couldn't remake it, but we had destroyed hundreds of thousands of pounds worth of money. It felt *good*. We decided to do more. Didn't realise that Ra was on a countdown, just thought this was how he rocked. We did six more sculptures till it all stopped, in between our other jobs. Each one of 'em internationally known works by a major artist. Abstract shit like my dad might have bought, or more neoclassical stuff that would have appealed to my mum. We put a lot of effort into making sure that we weren't seen. And we got loads of reviews for that work, so that got trickier, and we had to go further afield.

Ra was on the way out. Knew it for three months, since the day I asked him to leave calling cards. His MP3 beyond-the-grave message to me made it all too clear. Right from the start he was going to take me for what he could and get rid of me when I was of no more use. Sell me out to the police as a fall guy, or get me into crack, or whatever. That had been his pattern in recent years, like an evil Doctor Who. Get a sidekick and rinse 'em of all that they had. When they're no longer useful, get another screwed up kid with some resources and do the same. But they'd always been a bit of disappointment, got too fucked up too quickly. I was the first person who'd properly got into it and showed some mettle. Or perhaps that's how he thought about 'em, so he could allow himself to do it to 'em. Nevertheless, his voice told me how he had enjoyed his last season with me.

"I actually had a laugh. I had forgotten what that was like. Funny how death is the cure for everything."

He said he had no-one. He'd decided to spare me the usual complete rinsing, and on top of that the message went on, "It's time to fold. You can't take it with you. The first cards I got dealt when I was born were shit, and so was this last hand. I got fuck all on the flop from the doctor. I'm not betting on carrying on. It'll get too messy and undignified and I don't want that bullshit. I enjoyed playing the last few hands with you. You can have the stack I've accumulated. It's only fair. You've done the one thing I really did need you to do. You've killed me. Thanks for that… I jibbed it up on that roof. Didn't want that to happen again. Now get back to mastering the vibrations."

Everyone was partying. It was the twenty-seventh of July, two thousand and twelve. It was promising to be a good few weeks. The Olympics were kicking off and most of this country's plod was up in the East End. It was great news about the security company fuck-up too. More police pulled up to the smoke. Joy. The weather had turned out better for robbing, too. It had been pissing it down for months. Not so much fun in the wet when you're dealing with live cables. The last few days had been magic. And we'd had a lot of fun thieving stuff together. Now we were going for gold. Though I didn't yet know it, we approached what was to be our final target. *The Allegory of Metal* (alternatively known as *Property is War)*. It was huge. A technical masterpiece in bronze, by the roadside in the extended gardens of a stately home. It had been created by some modernist git that my father would have loved. It had various sectors, each suggested to me a different quality of metal, and its history. For example, there were chunks that seemed to me like they may have been supposed to be symbolic of different periods – bronze, iron, steel and uranium ages, and a zone that seemed to be connected to money and value, part of it looked like it had been made of millions of different types of coins glinting in the silver moonlight like a pirate's hoard. Another section of the sculpture seemed to be representative of conflict. It had long purposefully phallic objects sticking out of it that seemed like swords, pikes, guns and missiles.

Ra had got hold of a different vehicle, with a sizeable crane on the back. A Hiab. He made me wear chunky protective gloves.

"Touch nothing anywhere without these on." He insisted.

I thought that was because he'd robbed the vehicle, which was another skill I picked up from him. There was a large can of petrol in the back, intended for me to torch it when we'd done. Nice of him to think about getting rid of the evidence. When he told me what the fuel was for, I had no idea that I was going to have to do it without him. There was a bike on the back as well, I didn't think about that till I started to torch the lorry, but he'd thoughtfully provided me with a way to get home. It was nearly light by the time I'd cut the massive artifact free, had it chained and ready. Ra wanted me to have a go at operating the knuckle-boom. The loader crane was this hydraulically powered articulated arm fitted to the wagon. The operator had to move around to be able to see the load and so it used a portable cable-linked system to control the machine. I was working it. It was fun, standing next to the stabilising jacks, moving the tons of *Allegory*. It dangled in the void of the sky. My view was obscured. I was used to following Ras instructions, I had no reason to think he was standing, or even laying directly underneath a huge dead weight when he shouted out, "Dan, release the load. Now! For fucksake. Now!"

I did what I was told. There was a thud and Ra must have

croaked right there, he didn't make any more sound. There was just silence. The artwork must have crushed him completely. It was flat to the ground. He would have died almost instantly. I looked around for where he'd gone. Thought he was pissing about, pranking me. Hiding under the truck. But he was nowhere. The Alchemist had been transmuted. He sent a parcel to the house in Jimmy's End. It arrived two days after he died. I was expecting the police to show, pretty certain that I must have left some clue behind. Ra's mysterious death had made the TV and everything. I was really, really, really needing some coke, trying to forget that, by looking at the Olympic coverage. When the door knocked hard, my sphincter shrank to the size of a matchhead. But it was only the postie requesting a signature. In the brown envelope was a key, a Northampton address written by hand on a scrap of paper with a little hand-drawn map. It was over near the Racecourse. The package also contained a memory stick with his MP3 message on it. I expected his lockup to be like a breaker's yard, but it was very tidy and sparse. In it was a newish Land Rover with the paperwork, keys and a full tank, but no drugs that I could find anywhere. I was so pissed off I nearly didn't notice a couple of crates in the vehicle that contained what looked like gilded poker chips. When I looked closer it became clear that it was tens of thousands of pounds-worth of Krugerrands.

Screw the gold, I'd bring the bastard back and carry on if I could. Despite everything. I miss him. Love is probably the toughest thing of all.

THEIR ORIGIN

was in genetic experiments

a vast egg

tough brown fibrous exterior

somewhat like a gigantic coconut

inside many other pods with hard shells

they all burst out of the big egg together, simultaneous

as distinct types

singing frog-like creatures

female pigs, vocal and violent

 a chef, talking in Swedish

LIVING LIGHT

You are living on light. The doctor did not understand. Food is not necessary. Water is not necessary. You comprehend this now. The doctor did not. Robert should not have involved him. You are not ill. Just a bit cold. A bit disconnected. A period of adjustment is to be expected. You are living on light in accordance with your true will. The only food you need now is pure cosmic energy. Pranic nourishment. Breath.

Breatharianism found you on an internet chat site. Someone by the name of Celestial Body was singing its praises. When you first read about it you laughed. Surely it's not possible to live without eating? These people must be pranksters, con-men, or deluded. You and Robert both thought that. But it was just so fantastical you had to find out more. The more you looked into it, the more it became obvious that this was the ultimate way to live without cruelty. You wanted it so badly to be true that nothing had to die so you could live. That nothing would end. Funny to think about wanting anything so badly now. You do not even want to sleep anymore. Now that you're living on light you want for nothing. Robert said that you were talking shit. That you were doing a great deal of violence to yourself because of your hatred. But you would not kill anything, would you? No, not again. You were living entirely on light and Robert didn't understand. But then Robert never understood.

Even though you no longer eat, sometimes you like to look at food. It is only to be expected, your habits are difficult to break. You are alive on light, but there is further you can go. You are standing at a gas cooker, looking into a saucepan, watching frozen peas move in boiling water, defrosting as they spit and surf around in the anxious liquid. They spin seriously fast. Little green worlds. Dead now of course.

Robert has gone. He told you that he could not take it.

He feels guilty. He's still eating the life out of things. You are too bright, too bright for his eyes. You are standing at a gas cooker watching the only food that you have in your house, beautiful peas, peas you will not eat. You are owing money. You are orbiting the sun. Your mother died in childbirth. You never knew her. You are breathing in and out. You are subject to gravity. You are made up of beliefs. You are made up of cells, made up of molecules, made up of atoms of elements, made up subatomic particles. Your father is also dead. You have no other family. You are put into categories of location, age, race, culture, gender, sexuality, class, personality, finance, taste and size. You are subject to opinions. By coincidence, a particle of iron in the haemoglobin currently in your eye formed in the same dead distant star as a couple of particles in the peas. They were transported to just below the surface of this planet by a meteor two hundred and fifty million years ago. That sun has been dead for three billion years. Seven people in your street lost their first tooth on Tuesday, April the seventh. Yesterday you saw twenty-three people whose ancestors were from Finland, but you did not realise. Some of the water in your pan was once in the belly of a tyrannosaurus. Other water molecules also about to boil within the pan have recently been unfrozen after twenty thousand years in a solid state. Do they enjoy their liquid freedom? As an ocean manifests currents and tides, as it is observed over time, so you manifest many patterns and behaviours that flow obliquely through your life, and you are as aware of these patterns as the sea is aware within its wet infinity of each ebb, each wave impact. Over your life you will manifest many simple echoes, tendencies, themes, symbols. You will not become aware of them and will be blind to most of them forever. Sometimes you may get intimations. You may sense some freaky pattern. Seven people called Celia in a week. You suddenly start seeing pickled onions everywhere. Your mother was called Celia. But it slips away and you tell yourself you're wrong and the pickled onion stuff is just you and there is nothing to it; and it sort of feels like there is something hovering beyond conscious expression, you just do not manage to put your finger on it. That is all. It is there. If only you could sort of let the thought manifest… make the connection. But how the hell do you do that anyway? And you start thinking about all the things you have devoured, all the life you have consumed, and that now you are living, living on light and nothing need ever die again…

Just a bit cold, a bit disconnected. Robert has gone. The carcinogens and the toxins and the pollutants are going too. You are being cleansed. The vibrations have changed. And you have changed. Becoming lighter and lighter.

You began writing an alliterative composition with a lipstick. Do you remember? So far there are only five words in it, though they are repeated many, many times.

Meaning making monkey maybe mad.

Monkey making meaning maybe mad.

Mad monkey making meaning, maybe.

Meaning maybe making monkey mad.

Largely an autobiographical work. It remains unfinished. Robert thought it was about him. But you did write it on his car, didn't you? You should have expected his reaction. He never liked you writing. You do not know where that piece is going anymore. You do not know where it has gone. Driven away.

But every day, as the peas boil, at 11.23, I stand here and think about the ending.

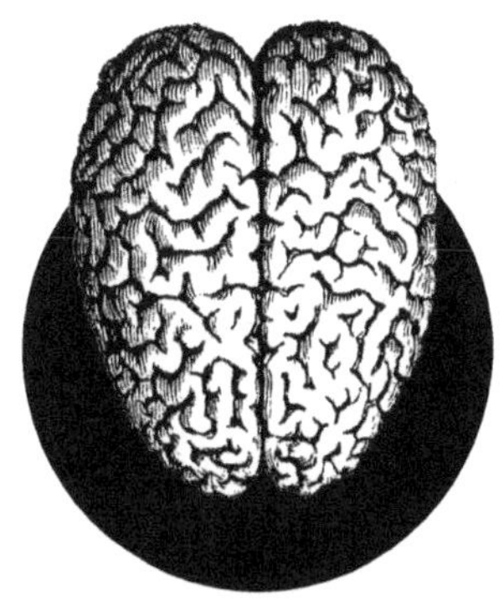

EVIDENCE OF SOMETHING

The main part of each word was sprayed from an ordinary matt-black aerosol paint can that was recovered from the scene. The highlighted capitalised text, was written out in the suspect's own blood using their index finger as a paint brush. The words found scrawled on the bedroom wall of the house were

SympTOm SpREADing TheORy
SurMOUNTing IlluSIONary AdVERSEness

BraIns braINs bRAINs
brAin reSEArchers
diviSEEs
thousANDfold arCANe lionHEARted arMADa
oVERSEe examINation
algorithmicALLy

MaTHEmatically comPASSIONate
straightFORwardly consTRUEd conSCIENCEs
scrutINise, apprAise
beWILDerment onomatoPOETICALly proLIFErating
durINg joYOUsly
insIStent
rePRESENTations

ReSENTment besTOws dANGERous mUSic
antiTHETical instRUCTIONs
interVENTions,
clANDestine phRASEs overinFLATing
– unsympaTHISing –
comPELLed, tramMELLed
ramPAGEr,
psychasTHENia encouRAGEd phONetically

AcKNOWledge dyspONESia's slOWNess.
FoMENTATIONs – hAREbrained fEVERs
contriBUTing indiviDUALity

PhONEme dISorders thUNDERous syNOnyms –
disILLUSIONed,
shortcHANGing sIMPLICITies
unAUTHORised inFORmation – dimorpHISms
comPENSating manOEUVREs

THE BOOK OF LOVE

"The philosophers have only interpreted the mind in various ways, the point however is to change it."

Major Joe Williams, Psychological Operations briefing 2003.

I was a man in the land of Af whose name was Joe. I was neither perfect nor upright. I was not one who feared God. Nor did I eschew Evil. Dual delusions that my brother perpetrated unto the people of our land. I lamented and cursed him unto his face for his stone-age beliefs. Thomas, my own twin. Double helices exact, but how different two could be who look and sound as one. Yet we were similar in our wroth; and I am escaped alone to tell thee of it.

I am my brother's keeper, his memory now within my own. My punishment is greater than I can bear. He could speak with the tongue of an angel, or bring the fear of God boiling in the blood of many who heard him resound. He would bring them unto his Lord. In tents across the land they would kneel and be healed. I had enough of him going on about God. I joined the army to get away from him.

I was a man in the land of Ir, on State business. In the Homeland my brother worked as a Shepherd for the Lord. We met as little as we could. He knew not of my work. Now I see our ways were most similar. I also dealt out persuasion. Our methods, if looked at with clear, cold eyes, are not so different. He got his converts the same way that I got intelligence, as I have come to appreciate. Care should have been taken, I suppose. He scared his sheep to save them. The difference being he kept them scared afterwards, separated them from their old group. When my job was done, I moved on. Stress is the key. I impair the detainees' judgments.

I like to play with little things, mix my signals. That's why I have the enemy flag on my keyring when administering the hardest slap to them they are ever likely to feel. In interrogation, I have no weaknesses. They do not know where they are or at what time of day. Make them anxious. Lie to them. Prolong the tension. We are looking for the transmarginal situation. So we are creative with it. We have all sorts of ways. Until Pavlov's little dogs bark and tell us what we want to know. Sometimes they wet themselves and sometimes they cry, and sometimes it goes so far that a man's beliefs will slip suddenly into total reverse. They will tell you anything then. They come to love Big Brother. The easiest way to break a proud religious man is to sexually humiliate him. Then make him defile his God. Hence the photos from such places as Abu Ghraib; they are for taunting purposes and have an acceptable military value. The grunts, they just carry the can. At least we did not torture their families in front of them, like the last lot. I had something else in mind for my brother. At our father's funeral I made the challenge, half in jest. My brother's sermonising provoked me. I had seen men renounce their Gods. He would too. It was simple. He rose to this challenge. It was as if we were children again. He had never forgiven me for being five minutes older than he. As a child he was practised in ways to trap me. Perhaps he trapped me still. For he demanded that I administer the test. I told him in two weeks his God would leave him. Perhaps he foresaw the outcome, loved me more than I knew.

I was a man in the land of my father. We went to the mountain, where we had gone as children. I put my brother to the test. The Chinese get good results with essay writing and group work over long periods. We in the West are in more of a hurry, subject to the whims of fashion.

My brother said, "The Lord have mercy upon your soul."

I then cuffed him in a very awkward position. Tied his hands up behind his back, placed a hood over his head and left him for 36 hours on the cold floor of a cellar, with nothing for company except the thrash metal music of Slayer playing, 'Reign in Blood' on a loop until its batteries died. I thought that would soften him up. He was in such a position that if he fell asleep it would cause him excruciating pain. For the first time in my life the enemy inspired sympathy in me. I tried not to think about my brother's suffering. While he agonised, I spent my time walking on the mountain reflecting on my life. I could not sleep. I should have terminated the mission then, or brought in assistance. I was proud. I did not. I was preparing for the bible study phase. I checked my biblical expertise as I walked. I would show Thomas that his knowledge of the book was not as good as he thought it was. That would undermine a core belief of his. It was a standard technique, but very effective; show them who's boss. He would be stressed and therefore forgetful. The cards would always fall for me on the flop. We would test each other on the bible and if he got it wrong I would give him an electric shock. And if I got it wrong I would undo one of his bindings. I started. He got it wrong straight away. The answer was the Book of Revelation and I was sure he knew it. He laughed. I hit him with the bare cables. As he writhed, I screamed, "Where is your God now?"

He said, "It's my turn to ask the questions."

I should have stopped then, had a rest. Taken that little bit of power away from him, but I did not. I suppose now I am grateful. For the first time in this kind of situation I lost my grip.

He asked his question, "According to Matthew, what did the Lord say upon the cross?"

And I knew as he asked it, he was giving me an easy one on purpose so that he would stay as he was. He was showing me that he was stronger than me, that he was prepared to suffer for his God.

And I answered, "My God, my God, why has thou forsaken me?"

Thomas smiled. Then I asked another and he got it wrong straight away, so I applied the wires. The pattern continued for three hours. He found it increasingly difficult to ask questions. It seemed his knowledge of the good book was gone, wiped. Although even then I felt things might not be as they seemed. I continued nevertheless. After some time, I thought I detected signs of a change. Thomas seemed to actually be struggling to get them right and began to look genuinely distraught. I was prevailing, but with this intuition came increasing sympathy for my brother. It was getting harder for me to apply the wires. I was no longer shouting "Where is your God?" as frequently as I had done at the beginning. As my respect and sympathy rose for him and his beliefs, his health began to fail. I was trapped with him; I could not leave him and regain my advantage. Thomas suffered a heart attack, I think, from what he said of the symptoms. Thomas told me that he would die. He closed his eyes. I was not sure whether to believe him. I began to examine him. I was increasingly filled with love for him. At the same time, I did not want to stop the procedure. I did not want him to die. I did not want to lose. I was tired. I was anxious. Frantic. I had done this all wrong. He opened his eyes, so much like mine. He fixed them upon me and said, "You were right, Joe. There is no God." And died in my arms, just like that. And as I held him, I felt the light and fear of the Lord fill me up. I knew that my brother had lied for me and died for me to save me from damnation. I became sure. Filled with the knowledge that there was a God Almighty and that Thomas had said those words to bring me to him. I would be saved.

As my brother has shown me, any means are acceptable that bring you to the Lord. And the Lord have mercy on my soul, that the work of my brother now falls to me.

ONLY ONES (REPRISE)

A deteriorating high street in evening rain. Relentlessly coated with grubby splashes, a wreath of mummified flowers. It is tied to a traffic island's railings and bleached by weather. A forgotten tribute to an anonymous casualty. Cars halt at a battered traffic light. Brake lights burn. The road, a blade of obsidian reflecting smudged pools of congealing blood-light. Oncoming traffic sprays out wet Doppler waves, rhythmic white noise, a mechanical ocean – becoming the static crackle of a between-frequencies radio. Its tuner is hunting for a coherent signal that may lie hidden in the endless cosmic fizz. The receiver picks-up babbling voices, screaming car horns, distant raptor calls, a mechanical toy; sounds of a jungle, of a hospital, desperate laughter, cold sex.

Nicotine fingers tune a bruised analogue radio. Twist its dial. Move a battered aerial. One wrist manacled by a tatty carrier bag. The receiver picks up signals, gets noise from everything it points at, but no clean transmissions.

The man with the bag and the radio is in his mid-to-late thirties. He is thin, dirty, wet. Passers hurry by avoiding contact with his hungry eyes.

Grey sky. A rod of silver probes damp air. Fully extended, the radio's aerial twists, divining chiseled judgmental faces leering down dark from the boiling clouds. Chasing the decaying signal, the man runs forward, head down, avoids eye contact with the grimaces staring down from the sky. Stronger, a new noise cuts in. The man swings the radio around, stalks the waveform along the path. His eyes briefly come alive as they follow the antenna.

There is a purer clearer sound now. The sound of words.

"Houston. We have a problem."

A tatty poster, pasted on top of many other ancient posters. The man's mucky face blank now as the aerial touches on the steel-armored window of a derelict shop. *Contact.* The poster's psytrance graphics include the red disk of a UFO.

The radio sound becomes clearer still. "Houston? Do you copy?"

Flickering red/amber/green time-lapse traffic lights strobe. Catch the man, hypnotize him, condense an hour into five seconds.

A blast of a sine wave. One thousand hertz. It cuts out all other sound. It screams loud enough to rattle teeth in passing heads. The man turns dizzily in the direction of this urgent tone. Aerial extending, searching towards the noise's epicenter – a street bin some distance away.

The man walks tentatively towards the bin as the sound dies to a hum.

An old woman, tidy in a coat and hat, wearing a hearing aid. She is pushing a trolley, stacked high with domestic items. On top of the pile is a circular light, shaped like a spacecraft from a 1950s film. The woman moves past the bin to enter the charity shop. She struggles awkwardly with her belongings as she negotiates the door with the trolley.

The man's radio is perched precariously on the edge of the bin. The man is rummaging rubbish intently. He stops. Looks up. The spaceship lamp visible from the street through the shop door-window. The door has closed. The woman is inside. The radio produces noises. "Danger, danger! Will Robinson."

Inside the charity shop an assistant is so excited by the elderly woman's delivery that she becomes wrapped up in searching through the donations.

Out on the street, the man is rummaging in the bin again. He pulls out a piece of a jigsaw. Examines it. Puts it in his pocket. He struggles with his carrier-bag handcuff. He tries to remove a jigsaw box from the bag. The box drops spinning, back-flipping to the floor. Its two halves come adrift, spraying pieces all over the wet ground as it falls. The box-lid face up. It is illustrated with a cartoon of the man. He is smiling, clean and healthy. The man sits down in the middle of the street. He tries to assemble the jigsaw where it has fallen.

Brisk legs walk by, ignoring, avoiding.

The jigsaw is part-assembled. It pictures the man, but there are many gaps. Part of the mouth is missing. There is a hole in the forehead. His hand takes the piece that he found in the bin out of his pocket. He places it into the jigsaw.

The jigsaw face now has a beaming smile.

A hasty pedestrian in work boots walks over the jigsaw puzzle, kicking pieces *harum-helter-topsy-skelter-turvy-scarum* bits fly out across the drenched concrete path, jumble their meaning.

One jigsaw piece, the newly discovered smile, goes further than the rest.

The man scrambles desperately after it.

The old woman leaves everything in the shop, other than the trolley. She slips away from the still-distracted assistant; back out of the door she came in through.

On the street, the jigsaw still remains part-assembled, showing a robot now. The puzzle piece with the smile displays a metallic mouth. The man, with stilted mechanical moves, jerks this piece back into the picture. The box lid, face up, flickers between the images of the healthy man smiling and the bulky robot.

The old woman reaches down to the man who is sitting on the ground in the wet. A wad of notes in one of her hands, a purse in the other. She passes the cash down to the man. He takes a piece of jigsaw; it is slightly larger and brighter than the others.

The radio crackles to a crescendo, then cuts out.

The man sits on the ground surrounded by scraps of paper, torn-up photos and a manky old Tupperware sandwich box rammed full with more scraps of photos, bits of paper and dog-ends.

The world through the old woman's hearing aid, ambient sounds slightly distorted, muffled birdsong, the distant hiss and rumble of cars on carriageway.

The old woman moves slowly, goes to return her purse to the bag. Stops. Puts the purse in her coat pocket and throws the handbag into the bin. Photos, a mirror, hairbrush, tissues, spill into the rubbish from the bag.

The old woman walks away.

The man stands. He moves towards the bin. Places the radio on the edge. He retrieves the bag, scoops in the belongings. The radio picks up a strong new signal. Many voices whisper incoherent warnings. The man struggles to pick up the radio, at the same time he tries to keep hold of the jigsaw and the handbag. Faces of strangers stare. A police car inches by.

Louder now, the radio broadcasts anxious jabbering glossolalia.

Stuck at the bin, the man works himself into a frenzy to budge his heavy robot feet. The old woman slowly getting further away. He manages to move. He gets away from the bin. Puts the handbag over his shoulder, steps jerkily after the old woman.

The radio broadcast fades.

Up above him on a pedestrian crossing the red man glows. A sticker with a fading scarlet UFO is stuck on the control. His fingers hesitate above the metal button. The red man. Heavy feet. A blurred trail of old women persists into the red, red distance.

The beep beep of the traffic light disrupts the radio. Ambient sounds move to the fore. The rain is starting up strong again. In distorted bursts, the radio fades out.

The man places one hand over his eyes. Darkness. Feet lighter now; they shuffle. With his hand over his eyes he is able to cross the road. He follows the old woman.

The radio plays something rhythmic that might be music.

The old woman arrives at a supermarket. She goes inside. She picks up a basket, puts it over her arm. She manoeuvres the basket and her trolley through the shop. The man enters the supermarket. Frantic radio-noise bombards him. He steps further into the shop.

The radio stops dead. Silence.

The old woman reaches the alcohol aisle. A security camera captures the man eating a cheese and onion pasty. He stands in front of a shelf full of pies. A hovering security guard hesitates. At the checkout, the old woman notices what is happening with the growing group of security people and the man. She looks away.

Security circle, then move in around the man. They force him towards the checkout with intimidating, eyeless stares. They do not touch him or talk to him. The old woman lets the man go in front of her at the till. The man's face blank. The old woman's mouth moves slow and silent.

The sounds of the radio begin again, scream to a crescendo.

The woman and the cashier coated by billows of red foaming mist, like exhaust.

Then silence. The fog disperses. The old woman speaks again. This time he hears.

"I'll pay."

She takes the remaining money from her purse. She pays for his pie. In her basket, bottles of vodka and packets of painkillers.

The man moves slightly away towards the exit. The cashier happily runs the pills and vodka through the scanner. The security guards glare, back the man out of the shop. They follow him to the door. The old woman moves past them with her trolley.

Out on the evening street, the guards stare at the man. He pulls his jumper over his head. The old woman looks at the man and moves off with her trolley. The man tags behind her at a distance. His head completely covered by the jumper.

The woman moves further away, her eyes downcast.

He follows her into a housing estate. He loses her. Radio silence.

Inside her tiny flat, the old woman's hands pull back a net curtain. She watches the man out of her window. She hears the muffled sounds of her sparsely furnished flat through her hearing aid as she moves around inside the building. Rectangular patches of colour mark the walls where paintings have been recently taken down. She gets out the pills and vodka from her trolley.

The old woman goes back to the window. She looks at the man who now sits on the ground outside in the Lucozade glow of a streetlight.

She puts on her coat. She goes out into the rain. The man has sat down in shit and broken glass. He is trying to put the jigsaw together. The old woman reaches down to him.

He stands.

He hands back her bag.

Hundreds of pills falling soundless, landing in a kitchen bin.

The man sleeps in a chair. A cup of tea beside him.

Her handbag on the draining board. The old woman is drinking a cup of tea while watching a bottle of vodka empty out. It is on its side in the sink. Clear fluid glugs out of its opening, flows off down the plughole.

He wakes. He looks at the woman. She hands him a plate of food, then picks one up for herself. The man begins to eat.

Emply plates.

The man stretches out peacefully.

The woman sits at a table putting a jigsaw together.

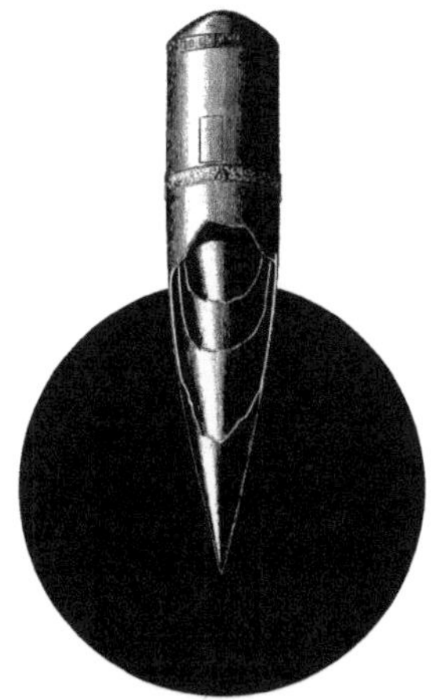

NOWASWILL

Our body is being preserved. With our will we are going now to childhood and are leaving the body. With our will we are going now to where we are being born and we are as our growing up. With our will we are going now to the town. With our will we are withholding the breathing. Now as will is Nowaswill.

It is as we are willing it. Here we are growing up. Now is here in darkness. We are being eight, nine, ten. We are being as now is, all as one.

We are fearing the dark gaps between entering rooms and turning on the light. We are knowing a tremendous fearing. In the absence of light, we must not on any account be breathing. This is learning.

Radiation, so potent in darkness. We are knowing that the light is off and we are in mortal danger. Radiation sickness is killing us. The light is being turned on and we are safe.

We are practising holding the breathing under the blue Radox water of a bath. The word Radox is reminding us of radiation.

Entering a dark room, we are knowing that there is radiation. No fearing now the light is off and we are waiting for sleeping, as a landing light is always on.

Monsters are existing. They are living in our wallpaper. Wizards are speaking to us as we are watching the patterns. Their faces in the curtains. There is something under the bed. We are hearing a heart beating. Common child thinking forms. Child we are being, and man.

These notions are worrying us. They are worrying us more in our own bedroom and the breathing is not being held to stop them. We are being terrified of nuclear war. This is involving radiation too, but it is somehow much worse, much worse. A story is being told about the very exciting thing old people are being involved with called The War. In The War, two cities are going. Two cities are going bang.

We are seeing one of these cities. We are as we are thinking. We are as with a nuclear bombing and the city is being not. We are as with thinking forms, here and for always as everything is for always in Nowaswill. A high fence with barbed-wire, and behind it being is nothing.

Nothing save only for darkness being. Behind the fence no city is and yet is. Behind the fence a dark wind is blowing not. On the side that is being in daylight, guards in olive drab are walking. Behind the wire no one is going. Behind the wire the bomb is meeting the city. There is here and here is there in Nowaswill.

As we are laying in the bed we are hearing the sirens of the hospital, growing nearer and nearer, moaning in pain. As man we are ignoring, as child we are hearing, as child and man we are in Nowaswill. The death wind is blowing. A fire alarm is sounding. A terrifying echoing of the four horsemen and their forewarning four-minute klaxon. We are waiting for the bomb to be dropping. Fearing is now. Fearing is now being absolute. Fearing is now being absolute and we are breaking away from the body. Fearing is now being absolute and we are breaking away from the body into Nowaswill. This is learning.

We are holding our breathing as we are going into the middle room and its lighting is flickering on. A presence, the personality of smells, the maliciousness, or friendliness, of the furnishings and the carpet and the wallpaper and the ornaments, the playing of light on the walls.

We are breathing and things are being as with breathing. The breathing is being held. Nowaswill is. Here is everything and everything is here as one.

We are breathing and things are as with breathing and as with fearing and as with the body and as with the terrifying echoing.

And we are visiting other houses. We are hiding bits of junk under wardrobes and in air-vents. We are hiding things. We are finding the hidden things. We are hiding the hidden things.

We are finding the world is what we are knowing. No evaporating if well hidden. We are deeply uncertain of the nature of the world so we are performing this experiment, this ritual. We are hiding the base of an Easter egg box, a piece of old newspaper and some stones. Here we are learning.

And holding the breathing in a room is defending us from radiation. We are not being in the room in the way of no learning. We are being in the room with learning. We are being in the room that is with Nowaswill.

The testing. We are discovering hidden things. We are seeing the minor details in the world of breathing, the things we are forgetting. We are seeing if the things we are forgetting are disappearing.

Fearing of radiation, at least fearing that is manifesting itself in the holding of the breathing, is being inspired by a play we are seeing on telly. A woman working in a nuclear power-station is stealing plutonium, taking it home and eating it and bathing in it and rubbing it in her hair. She is being a protest. It is scaring the shit out of us. We are fragmenting. The message is being made clear. Nothing is being foolproof or safe in the world with breathing.

Radiation is leaking out through the darkness. We are developing the simple way, the learning way, it is being our defending. The light is turning off and we are holding the breathing and are as one.

We are being born into a world. We are discovering that it is going bang. We are learning defending measures against the invisible. We are learning. We are learning. We are collecting pictures of missiles and learning their names, Minuteman, Polaris.

We are always placing these items in particular locations in other homes. Only we are knowing that they are there. We are being thrilled by the secret relationship between the wardrobe and the empty Easter egg box. Our own secret ordering of the universe. This is our learning. This is how we are replacing the world with breathing. Nowaswill is what we are calling it, as child, as man, as one.

While we are breathing not, and are being Nowaswill, we are feeling such urges, to be sculpting the secrets connecting between things. The box and wardrobe, as with the air-vent and stones, are our learning.

We are reading that children's games are reflecting their environment. We certainly are finding this true of the child we are. We are enacting the ceremonies that is the learning. This is Nowaswill. The hiding, the finding, are learning. As a child we see, and see not as man. Only in Nowaswill do we see as man, as child, as one. The body is being left.

In holding the breathing, we are trying. Practising. We are holding the breathing in order to be controlling the radiation. We are discovering Nowaswill.

We are forgetting nuclear wars and radiation and darkness. We are learning and learning.

We are holding our breathing. We are always stepping out of a normal room, into a real room. A room full of a room's actual significances, into the meaning of Nowaswill. We are stepping into the other. We are doing it. And doing it. And doing it. We do it and are in the other for an eternity. The burning lungs are calling us. But always less of us is with the world. We are needing, we are needing, we are needing Nowaswill.

The world without breathing we are calling Nowaswill. It is as with the world of breathing, in most respects. We are in Nowaswill, but are being not with the body. The less the body is feeling. We are being in Nowaswill forever. And yet we are and the body is not being forever. Yet we are being with the body and the body is not forever being. And yet is. We are feeling less and less of it. We are knowing the feeling of without feeling and are withholding the breathing. A being body is preserved.

THINGS OF CONSEQUENCE

(Written in partnership with Barry Hale)

EXT. A BEACH ON THE ISLE OF SHEPPEY – DAY

Summer Sounds – seagulls, ice cream vans, the hum of rotary mowers, distant waves, the goings on of holidaymakers on this windswept estuary island.

Far below us, at the foot of the cliff, a striped, over-large umbrella – a sunshade's perfect multicoloured circle over the beach of dirty yellow sand.

Feet protrude. One pair. Shockingly white. Naked toes involved in sand games beside two sandcastles. HAROLD, a man of about forty-five in horn-rimmed spectacles and a straw hat. Fifteen years ago, he could have been mistaken for Harold Lloyd. But this Harold has lost the innocent smile and his glasses have seen much better days. His nose is absurdly covered in a white sun-protection cream. His shorts and T-shirt recall Edwardian swimming costumes. He sits in a deckchair beneath the umbrella, reading an old tatty book. Constantly reassembling the loose pages, straightening them as they try to slip free from the broken spine. He looks up as the encroaching tide tickles his toes. He watches as one of the castles swells with water. It slowly crumbles.

His face is a battlefield of expressions – boredom, satisfaction and fascination.

THE SOUND of WASPS.

Harold is panicked from his inactivity. Phobic eyes shoot rapidly around his face, trying to focus as he follows the flight of the insects. He leaps from his chair, batting at the insects with his book. White pages fly free as he dances around the chair like a Keystone Kop. He slams the book closed. The buzzing stops.

He opens the book. A last gasp, a halfhearted buzz is quickly extinguished by a solid slamming of the hard covers once again.

The umbrella malfunctions, slams shut, squeezing Harold within it. Pages of the book fall from the trap as Harold struggles to fight his way out of the umbrella. He opens the umbrella, only to clumsily step into the frame of the chair. Harold hastily clambers out, hops, almost trips through it. Rips the cloth, breaks the wooden frame. He accidentally stamps on the remains of the surviving sand castle. He destroys it completely.

He drops what is left of his book.

White pages float away on the foaming tide.

He frees himself from the umbrella, from the ruins of the deckchair.

The SOUND of the WASPS starts up again. Angry.

Harold backs away from the book, abandoning it in the sand. He clumsily gathers his other effects. He retreats as rapidly as he can manage. The narrow beach is situated at the base of a steep cliff. The tide is coming in. The surf rolls up. The cliff face looms before him. A glimpse of the caravans parked along its edge peep over the lip. Harold, as hastily as he can, climbs the twisting path towards them.

EXT. CLIFFTOP – DAY

Reeds along the edge of the cliff wave in a strong sea breeze. Incidental music played on a Victrola is carried to us on the air.

Two holiday caravans, side by side, 1970s in design. Mundane. They perch on a rim of grass before miles of sparkling grey estuary water. Harold's straw hat peeps up over the cliff's edge as he climbs the last few steps of the path from the beach. He pants a little. Red in the face. Except for his white nose covered in sun cream.

The caravan door. Harold puts his belongings down outside. The Victrola music is clearer now. Harold pinpoints its source to the neighbouring caravan. It has an eerie yet nostalgic aura. It would not sound out of place as the incidental music in a Laurel and Hardy movie.

Harold fumbles with his keys. Walks up the metal step. As he pushes the key into the lock he pauses, as if sensing a presence behind him.

He turns, discreetly, in time to see. . .

. . .the curtain of the caravan opposite pulled tightly closed. A glimpse of white gloved fingers. Possibly a bowler hat shadowing a long horse-like face – in pain or alarm. . .

The cloth of the curtain is a solid dark grey. The ornaments, a vase of Tyrolean dried flowers, also grey. The world inside this caravan is black and white, like an old TV show.

The music stops.

Harold turns away, opens the door. He enters his caravan.

INT. HAROLD'S CARAVAN – DAY

He climbs up into the caravan.

A distorted face peers out of the dark interior. Bullseye red with a white nose. Gulls cry out. Harold screams silently. He recoils from the Munch-like face. Realizes it is his own – his distorted reflection is thrown back at him by a mirror he has left on the table.

He moves the mirror. He sheepishly wipes the remainder of the cream from his face.

He lights a gas ring in the kitchen area. Fierce blue flames burning. A pan of water placed on the ring. Two eggs dropped in water. An over-cranked sun goes down outside the lace curtained windows

INT. HAROLD'S CARAVAN – NIGHT

Harold lies in his bed asleep.

Strange yelps fill the night like the panicked cries of a half-human kookaburra– the sawing of heavy timbers, creaking, splitting and falling with a forest felling crash.

Harold wakes and removes his sleep-mask in alarm.

Silence.

Harold is wide awake now. . .

The sound of an acetylene torch being lit.

Human shouts fill the night. The sounds of furniture being

torn apart. The creaks, cracks and yelps of pain are loud, violent, hair-raising.

Harold pulls back his curtain. He peers through his window at the neighbouring caravan.

EXT. NIGHT THE OTHER CARAVAN

Nothing out of place.

The neighbours' van shudders violently. The curtains ripple. They billow open slightly for no more than a second. A glimpse of a shadow. A CORPULENT GENTLEMAN IN A BOWLER HAT WITH A TINY MOUSTACHE PERCHED BENEATH HIS NOSE wields a club above his head.

His target – another bowler hat bobbing in and out of view below him.

The curtain quickly closes, hardly long enough for the sight of the wild-eyed grimace of the murderous man inside to register.

INT. NIGHT HAROLD'S CARAVAN

Harold hides from sight, peeking occasionally through his curtains as the noises continue.

LATER, all is silent. Harold peers nervously out at his neighbours' caravan.

EXT. NIGHT THE OTHER CARAVAN

The sound of the gramophone starts again as if nothing has happened. It is a lonely, eerie sound by night. An under-cranked morning comes to the caravans as the music dies away.

EXT. OUTSIDE HAROLD'S CARAVAN – DAY

Harold sunbathes in his protective white cream. His back to

the sun, lying on a multicoloured towel, facing his neighbour's caravan. It's a quiet, bright, summer morning.

There is a squeaking noise. Harold looks up. The skylight in the caravan is being pushed up. Opened by a hand that seems to be gloved, or heavily bandaged.

There is a pained cry from inside. The noises of furniture being reduced to matchsticks cannot drown the cries.

Harold leaps up in alarm.

He hides around the back of his caravan. Peers around the corner with his glasses perched at the end of his nose. He hides and returns to look again, his face disappearing and returning like a nervous bird.

There is nothing to be seen.

Harold summons his courage and heads decisively towards their caravan.

He sticks his face against the nearest window. Then against each window in turn, faster and faster, but cannot see through.

The noises from inside begin again, more frenetic than before. The yelps wilder, more frequent.

The caravan rocks violently as Harold tries to peer inside, hitting him square on the forehead, breaking the brim of his straw boater.

He inspects the damage before replacing it on his head.

Harold hammers on the front door in outrage.

The noises cease. Harold listens at the keyhole. Stands boldly, meaning business, with hands on hips, waiting for the door to open.

He visibly deflates as he realizes no one will answer.

Starts to move as if to leave, hesitates, then steps awkwardly away.

He looks back as he reaches the corner of the van to check that no one has yet come to the door.

Hesitates. . .

Walks resolutely back to the door. . .

The violence resumes with as much force as before.

Harold grasps his hat to his head and runs.

EXT. DAY – BEACH

Seagulls wheel over sparkling water.

Harold makes a clumsy attempt to fish from the beach – he flicks his antique rod time and again into the surf to no avail.

EXT. DAY – HAROLD'S CARAVAN

Harold returns to the boot of his car to replace his fishing gear after a successful trip. In a storage net he has one miniscule flat fish that he has caught. He licks his lips in anticipation of the feast to come.

He hears the click of his neighbour's caravan door.

He drops to the ground, face next to fish. He peers beneath the caravan in time to see two feet in black boots step down from the van and walk away.

He trots nimbly round to the front of his neighbour's caravan to get a better view of them.

They are nowhere to be seen.

INT. NIGHT – HAROLD'S CARAVAN

The gramophone still plays. The needle has caught in a scratch. The remains of the tiny fish on the table – a doll's house fish-skeleton with the head intact.

Suddenly the screeching starts again. Harold jumps up.

Stands at the open door of his caravan.

EXT NIGHT – HAROLD'S CARAVAN

The skylight on his neighbour's caravan opens again.

Harold rushes to their caravan.

He bangs on the door. Inside, the gramophone is booted. The music comes to an abrupt end.

Silence.

He tries to peer through the curtains. The outlines of two men. Shadows, a tall thin one and a big round one. Both in bowlers

Harold rubs his eyes.

Harold adjusts his glasses.

Harold looks again.

The caravan's interior is entirely monochrome. The edges of furniture, the small patch of wallpaper, the fruit in the bowl, all are shades of grey.

Harold retreats from the window. He hears a faint sob, a whine, a near-animal but human whimper. He pauses. The whine becomes louder and more desperate.

Harold rushes back to his caravan. From the storage space beneath it he produces a ladder.

He puts the ladder up against his neighbour's caravan.

Climbs the ladder.

He slips, and slides down it, hurts himself. He bites his fist to restrain himself from crying out.

He tries again and climbs onto the van roof.

He stretches his neck to push his face deep into the open skylight.

He cautiously sticks his head right through the hole.

INT. NIGHT – THE NEIGHBOUR'S CARAVAN

Harold's head is inside the caravan. He hangs upside-down – a full colour face within a monochrome world.

Harold sees the Victrola, currently silent. Two bowler hats hang on the wall beside it. On the table, a discarded bow-tie and a normal tie. The caravan looks as if it hasn't been redecorated since 1931.

His glasses slide off. (With some difficulty) he manages to catch them, silently. He struggles to put them back on. Fails.

As they fall to the floor REVEAL two blurry male figures in black suits looming from the shadows towards the back of the caravan. One is large and round, the other tall and thin. The thin figure sits in a chair. The larger of the two holding something in a menacing fashion – we see it is a feather duster.

REVEAL the man in the chair's feet are naked.

Harold sheepishly smiles at them while hanging upside down from their skylight. He slips further in.

No amount of wriggling will save him now. Too far in to get out.

EXT. NIGHT – THE NEIGHBOUR'S CARAVAN

Harold's legs stick vertically out of the caravan.

His legs disappear as he is pulled inside

INT. NIGHT – THE NEIGHBOUR'S CARAVAN

Harold lands with a crash on his glasses.

The shadows of the two figures stand over him. Silent.

The demonic faces of the two men are dark, focused.

The two men reach down for him.

Harold looks at them both in terror.

As the thin man reaches for Harold's face fine jets of fierce blue fire erupt from each of his thumbs.

He fixes to burn out Harold's eyes. . .

. . .but the larger man lays a hand on his companion's shoulder. Taps him repeatedly and ushers him away.

He pushes the thin man into a corner with just the tips of his white gloved fingers.

He turns with a malevolent grimace to Harold, scuttling across the floor for safety.

EXT. NIGHT – THE NEIGHBOUR'S CARAVAN
Splintering timbers, the clang of iron cooking pans bouncing off fragile bone.

A new voice is crying inside now – Harold's.

The caravan rocks and teeters from the action inside. It sounds as if the heart of the van is being torn from its living wood and metal body.

Then silence.

A needle placed on a 78 groove.

We hear the Cuckoo Waltz start to play.

IT IS PROBABLY WORSE OUTSIDE

He wanted to be a clown.

Machinery continued to stamp out the product.

His bicycle stood against the corroding radiator.

The smell of burning plastic filled the air.

The monitor had called again.

The monitor had checked the production rate.

He sat at his post.

They would hold him to blame for the fall in production.

A fog of desperation enveloped him.

The monitor put away a stopwatch.

The monitor made another mark on the clipboard.

Machinery continued to stamp out the product.

He wanted to be a clown.

The monitor went away.

He sat at his post.

He smelt burning plastic.

The monitor returned with a supervisor.

The supervisor looked at a stopwatch.

His bicycle stood against the corroding radiator.

He looked down.

The supervisor made a mark on the board.

The supervisor and the monitor went away.

He looked at his bicycle.

He looked at the machinery stamping out product.

He got up from the chair.

He walked towards his bicycle.

The monitor returned.

The monitor saw that he was not at his post.

The monitor frowned.

The monitor made three marks on the clipboard.

He returned to the chair.

He looked down.

Machinery continued.

He sat at his post.

He wanted to be a clown.

He looked at his bicycle.

Desperation enveloped him, smelling of burning plastic.

He looked down

The monitor had called again.

The monitor had checked the production rate.

He sat.

They would hold him to blame.

He sat.

He sat.

He wanted to be a clown.

He got up from the chair.

He moved over towards his bicycle.

He turned quickly.

He sat back down.

The monitor returned.

The monitor gave him a form.

He looked at the floor.

He put the form in the jacket pocket.

The monitor went away.

He got up from the chair.

He turned quickly towards his bicycle.

He wanted to be a clown.

He removed his bicycle from the radiator.

He placed his bicycle near the exit flap.

He hesitated.

He returned to the chair.

Machinery continued to stamp.

He sat.

The monitor called again.

The monitor checked the production rate.

The monitor did not notice the bicycle.

The monitor put away the stopwatch.

The monitor made another mark on the board.

The monitor went away.

He got up from the chair.

He moved quickly towards his bicycle.

The monitor returned.

The monitor saw that he was not at his post.

The smell of burning plastic filled the air.

The monitor frowned.

The monitor made three marks on the clipboard.

Machinery continued to stamp out the product.

He returned to the chair.

The smell of burning plastic filled the air.

He looked down.

The monitor went away.

He got up from the chair.

He tried to place his bicycle back against the radiator.

The front wheel fell off.

He looked down.

The handlebars came off in his hand.

The monitor returned.

The monitor saw that he was not at his post.

He tried to return to the chair.

He slipped.

The monitor frowned.

The monitor made five marks on the clipboard.

He picked himself up.

He tried to return to the chair.

Blood leaked from his nose.

The monitor went away.

He tried to put the handlebars back on his bicycle.

The monitor returned with a supervisor.

The back wheel fell off.

He looked down.

The supervisor frowned.

The supervisor gave him a form.

Machinery continued to stamp out the product.

He smelt burning plastic.

The monitor gave him a form.

The monitor and supervisor went away.

Blood leaked from his nose.

He did not return to the chair.

He looked down at the bicycle.

His nose was red.

He looked at the exit flap.

Machinery continued.

He looked at the bicycle.

He looked at the exit flap.

The smell of burning plastic filled the air.

They would hold him to blame.

He looked at the exit flap.

He wanted to be a clown.

Blood leaked from his nose.

He looked at the exit flap.

He hesitated.

MURDER AT THE ALLOTMENT

Having originally resolved to hang myself anyway, it is quite fitting that I should be sitting here waiting to be escorted to the recently reinstated patriotic gallows. This week's dispatching is sponsored by a much beloved product, I believe. This cell is about the size of the hut where I planned to top myself. But the window is much smaller and there is not much to see of the outside world, in which I'm not really interested anyway. Never have been really. They weren't interested in me. I wasn't interested in them. Fair's fair. Not that the view from the hut was anything to speak of and what view there was, was more than obscured by an accumulation of filth and abandoned webs. Though possibly the webs weren't abandoned. I didn't really give them that much attention. Perhaps they were not webs at all but some fungal outgrowth. Possibly I have imagined the webs. The view from the window was probably just as hazy as my recollection of it. Maybe I have invented the webs to compensate for my lack of memory regarding the window specifically. I think not. There was a general presence of grime in the place, which was after all supposed to be used for a number of agricultural purposes. A layer of dust had, even before I had inherited the shack, become almost a kind of soil. Webs would not be out of place in a hut like that. All that could be seen out of the window, or in my memory of this view, was part of a tree that may have been an apple tree. And a small section of fencing. Though this is from the sitting down aspect, which was generally how I positioned myself when I was in the building, such as it was. It was as pleasant a place to have a smoke as any other. I wasn't much of a gardener. I kept up the appearance of being a member of the green fingered community, or at least I thought that I did, but the only thing I ever seemed to grow with any measure of certainty was older. The sitting down aspect was truly the one which I preferred and I am in this pleasing posture now in my cell. I'd sit in the hut in a worn deckchair, whose stripes had faded so much they were barely visible. Most things were barely visible in the hut. I would watch the glowing end of my rollie, hardly able to discern any movement through the filthy square of glass that looked out onto the immediate environment, which I was as interested in as anywhere else. As I have already indicated my interest was minimal. Golden Virginia rolling tobacco, a packet of green Rizla papers, a supply of tea and an adequate amount of soft toilet paper were my principal concerns. And Bill, let's not forget Bill, my first victim, or rather my last, so it would seem. I am getting ahead of myself and I probably haven't adequately made the distinction between my memories of the views from the window while sitting down and standing up. Perhaps I am making too much of it. After all, windows look out, or in, I suppose. I rarely looked out, or in, though them. Bill might have, but I doubt that. He wasn't the adventurous type. We shared use of the premises. We had two deckchairs and often used to sit and smoke together. He rarely spoke. I do not recall anything particular he ever said to me. He may have been a more enthusiastic gardener than myself. I'm not sure. For my part I cannot remember if I ever actually saw him labour over a patch of earth. I remember his wellingtons often collected mud between the tread, but this is not conclusive proof. As I've said, we had two deckchairs. We never sat in each other's. I suppose this was almost a ritual. I would never have dreamed of putting my arse onto Bill's seat and I suppose Bill did not want to put his arse onto my seat. Or perhaps he did. Perhaps he actually achieved this secret desire, by swapping the seats, while retaining their respective positions. I was never aware of it. It seems to me that Bill was an unadventurous type who would not have gone in for seat swapping. Though perhaps I should have asked him, cleared it up between us. Too late now though. He was the last one that I did, or rather the first. Or rather, I was as responsible for his actual death as for all the others, for which I am going to hang. As I have mentioned, I had resolved, in fact prepared, to hang myself. I had gone so far as to actually purchase a length of rope that looked up to the job. I was always there an hour before Bill. He would find me and deal with it in a way he thought appropriate. Perhaps he would at last pick up the courage to swap seats. I had planned it all out. Examined the height of the beam in the hut. Tested its strength. I was glad Bill would be there, who else would find me? Bill was my best friend. At least

I think that was his name. He didn't say a lot. I could have just started calling him that because we were never introduced as such. He was just in the shed when I moved in. He never said much. Perhaps he could not be bothered to correct my mistake. He may have preferred Bill to his actual name. The police called him Bill, though they could have got this from me. Officially Bill is good enough. It probably reads Bill on his headstone, if he has one. If indeed he was buried. These are the sort of details to which I don't pay attention, like the webs and the window. Bill himself, though I sat next to him for extensive periods, is a mere collection of indeterminate features to my mind's eye. Even when later I got him down, he landed face first, so I never got much of a look at his mug and there was never much light in the shed anyway. As I've said, I got rope. Nylon I think. It was quite expensive, but I wasn't saving for anything. Sod the expense. I don't know what brought it on. Why another amount of time with Bill was no longer possible. I feared my chair might soon give way. I feared Bill had swapped chairs. I feared many things. I had long ago given up any inclination to make any kind of noise in the world at large, to have my name in the newspapers and heard on the radio and television. And to have people I had never met write to me, or at least I thought that I had given up. Perhaps people I had not met had written to me. I am uncertain. I had bills I suppose, not Bill's but bills, invoices, expenses. I must have done. Certainly, I had an occasional anonymous correspondence, but nothing on the level I had hoped for. I was early to the allotment. I wanted to get it all over before that seat-switcher Bill put in an appearance. I paid the usual amount of attention to the path and weeds, and there was always the smell of a bonfire whatever time of day. But the details aren't there.

The days have become blurred in my memory so that all the seasons exist simultaneously. There do not seem to be that many specifics. There was a path. There may have been weeds. Yes, weeds there were. I was pleased with my weeds. Bird song was not something with which I ever established a rapport. Their language I did not understand. So I probably edited this pointless signal from my mind, though doubtless there may have been some. Distant cars too. Though I don't see how that matters now I come to mention it. I don't remember noticing any omens, though I was never previously prone to noticing any omens, nor have I been since. Even as I wait here to be hanged the world seems neither more, nor less, significant that it ever was. I held my rope and shuffled my way towards the shed. I might as well say here that the shed was constructed out of a timber frame over which corrugated iron was laid. The iron, I believe, was fastened with screws. Like any shed, I suppose. Though many are all of wood and some are mostly metal. Ours was one of the combination type, and serviceable it was too, for my purpose anyway. Its roof consisted of three strong beams. The central beam was the one over which I planned to pass the rope. Under which Bill would find me dangling. My plan rested very much on Bill finding me. This was my obsession. I didn't want to be dangling there any longer than I had to be. If he hadn't swapped chairs, well, it would have been different. But that bastard… Well, never mind that. I walked into the shed after fiddling with the lock, which was of the mortise type. I saw Bill. Well, I wasn't certain it was Bill, as I've said, I never saw him properly. He could, in fact, be a whole series of different individuals who I just happened to believe were the same person. Perhaps Bill is just my term for other people. I think not.

Anyway, Bill had foiled my delicately laid plan. Not only by being there early, but also by having suspended himself, prior to my arrival, by a nylon rope of a similar quality to my own, so I believed, from the most central of the three strong roof beams. This placed me in a quandary. A vital element of my scheme had been foiled by my acquaintance's action. Perhaps he, if he was a he, had also feared that the seats had been swapped. Who is to say? I hesitated. The beam would not support both our weights. It had to be the central beam. I thought that I had better cut him down and put myself in his place, but who would find us? Did I not owe it to my friend to alert the uncaring world to his demise? What was Bill? Would the world stop turning for anybody? Obviously, the git had upset my particular applecart, though I am not fond of apples and do not remember owning anything to transport them about in. If I had done, no doubt Bill would have managed to upset it, or swap it for another without me realising. But I wasn't any more affected by my plans being altered than I was by anything else. I sat down in one deckchair and put my feet upon the other, a luxury I had never enjoyed before, for they were both mine now I supposed. I rolled a cigarette. The roof creaked a bit I think as Bill swung gently. It was at this point (well not 'point', that sounds like there was a moment when really it was a gradual increase of feeling) my thoughts began to return to my youthful desires that had been disappointed and forgotten. Should I cut Bill down and string myself up? No. There was a way in which Bill could at last be of value to me. Bill my best friend, my passport to fame and its accompanying rewards. I put the rope down. I moved towards the tool drawer and found a pair of shears and got up onto the table, which I haven't previously mentioned because I had not recalled its existence. There was one. I'm sure of it, though it may have been only a desk. It was always too dark in there. The long and short of it is that I cut him down and he fell, landing on his face and knees, buttocks up. Many people have done worse things than sodomise a dead man to get themselves famous. I am sure of it. But it was clear to me that it would be a fairly simple procedure. I don't know why I was so certain that Bill was male. Not that you can't sodomise dead women. In fact, I am found guilty of it. But I was certain Bill was male. I believe that I had never had sex with a man before, or since for that matter. I'm sure that I only engaged in sexual intercourse on two other occasions. Both times with what I believe to be women, but they might have been men. Since both times it involved placing my penis into a mouth, I cannot be certain. I am certain that it cost me the equivalent of six ounces of tobacco and was a lot less fun than smoking. Ever since, whenever it got hard, I indulged in the five-knuckle shuffle. This is perhaps why my eyesight is failing me. Though this is no real loss. I don't feel guilty mind you, about masturbating, or sodomising my dead friend. Perhaps I would have felt guilty if Bill were alive. Perhaps not. Though I am glad that nature, as far as I can recall, did not really give me a passion for sodomising dead people just to get to sleep at night. No, luckily I've found simple masturbation quite adequate, puts me straight to sleep. Though when I first discovered wanking I was convinced that every dead person I had ever known, in the form of ghostly presences, would know that I was masturbating. Though during my intercourse with Bill I did not seem to mind whether he knew or not. Having sex with dead people, the forensic psych' tells me, was a way for me to come to terms with the delusion that dead people watch me masturbate. The shrink's a nut. He really thinks I killed all those people because my dead uncle used to watch me jerk off. He names a few Greek myths and thinks he's got to the bottom of it all. Sodomising was a longer procedure than you would probably have anticipated. I was a novice at such things. The clothes were quite difficult to remove and it took me a number of moments to get myself into the correct mood in order to carry out the act. Though friction is friction and it seems to do the trick. A bit messy, but that's sex pretty well summed up. Well, was it sex? I suppose that it was. Perhaps I even loved dead Bill. No, I never loved anyone. Not even myself. Though Bill, if that was the person's name, was probably the closest I have come to love. Though I speak about sex like I am an expert, I am not. For, as I have said, I have only had intercourse on three occasions that have fixed in my mind. Then only once without paying for it and that was with Bill, whom I may have loved. Though I am about to pay for this with my life. Anyway, I will not deny I felt some attraction to Bill and that I may have done what I did for other reasons, as the psychiatrist reckons. But if I was going to carry the can for the death of Bill I wanted to be sure that I did it properly and that was the sort of thing murderers did, according to the papers anyway. Not that I read them very often, or had taken much interest in them when I did. Tits don't interest me as much as they did, and the outside world is better off outside. Why read about it? They'd never read about me. Well until now. The next part I do not recall so well, or rather it all blurs into itself and I cannot disentangle it. My mind does not seem able to fill this space with any illusions. Any that I am aware of. But that's the funny thing about illusions, I suppose. Police are also hard to disentangle from one another. They were mostly different from Bill, but some could have been my old friend, and when I thought that I saw him I cried tears of happiness, though it seems I was mistaken. To be honest I am not sure if any of what I am saying is what happened, but I am as sure as most people, I suppose. Then most people don't sodomise their dead best friend. Or so I am told. I may be an unusual case. Though I was then certain I had killed no one I confessed to every crime that needed wrapping up. I did this, I believe, without any intimidation on behalf of the police, but of my own free will, if I have such a thing. The police were friendly enough, from what I recall of them. They left me locked up in places not too dissimilar from the shed, from which I had been removed eventually. I informed them, I think. I'm not sure how. Perhaps it was via the telephone. It would seem likely. Nine-nine-nine calls are free, I believe. It was a solicitor, or perhaps a police officer, or some mixture of these two roles, that first suggested the idea of film rights. I simply nodded at the suggestion, it fitted in with what I had hoped. I'm not sure how many people were involved, probably only one. It would seem likely. I had already been in the papers and on television, though this was something of an anticlimax. I forget why. My enthusiasm for a movie was only moderately higher than my enthusiasm for the outside world in general. My youthful desires had sunk back into aimless disinterest. Though, by the time they had made the film, I was more interested again. I wondered vaguely how they had interspersed my years in the shed with my fictional murder spree. I have seen the film. The ending is already shot. The execution. Jumping the noose somewhat, as I'm not yet quite dead, I believe. I suppose they think that I will not win a last-minute appeal for clemency. Reasonable enough I suppose, as

I'm not appealing. I have killed more people than anyone else ever captured, so it would seem. I am a superstar. The film was very revealing. It showed me many things I had forgotten about my life. And quite a lot about Bill's, though I forget exactly what happens. I have a lot of fan mail, I'm told. Though I pretend not to hear them when they tell me. It may only be one person who told me, or who tells me, though who can say? I cannot. I forgot that I was addicted to drugs and tortured animals. I forgot that the police finally managed to arrest me at the end of a hectic car chase. I forgot I knew how to drive. I forgot about my girlfriend with enormous breasts, who never suspected my activities. I forgot about the visions I'd had of Jesus. I forgot that I was the illegitimate son of a millionaire. The film seems certain of all these details, so they are probably true. I do not see why not. Just because I do not remember it that way, everybody else will. I don't remember very much anyway. The drug addiction, perhaps that would explain it. Though what you are actually supposed to do with crack remains a mystery to me, I think. From the film it would appear that you smoke it in some way, though I am unsure. I can still smoke my roll-ups. There's a special dispensation for those that are going to swing. I am glad of that. Though I didn't smoke them in the film. Perhaps I should stop. I just met the hangman, I think, okay chap. A double for Bill. Absolute spit. Perhaps he'll get there first, like Bill. I am a monster. It seems children are scared of me. I discussed rope with the hangman. I told him of my plans to kill myself, he said something about leaving it to the professionals. I think that was the gist of it. They wanted me to do a chat show. I think I said no. Though I don't know why. I'm tired of fame perhaps, probably that. The hangman said something about there being amateurs and professionals. I told him I had killed more people than him. He became silent. Though I don't see how it matters much. He gets to kill me after all, I suppose. Though I'm not sure where life ends and death begins. No, I'm not sure at all.

WIRCUS

An expressionless face. An expressionless face mirrored. An expressionless face mirrored in a metal hatch contained within the body of a machine without end. A mechanised array of articulated rubber-steel limbs that move together as if partly human within the carcass of an inorganic cetacean. A haphazard undead beast seemingly pulled from a toxic beach to be stored here in a dank windowless bunker, along with the debris from a monochromatic explosion at some kind of innovative fetish club. This machine never sleeps. Massive insectoid drones swarm around their queen. Feathered fans of fibreoptic lights emerge. Its viscera visible, a vast organism pinned out awaiting vivisection. A room dominated by shades of black, white or grey.

The Operator's finger draws a simple smiling face over their dull reflection in the oil that coats the hatch.

The hatch slides open. Beneath it lies a complex serpentine tangle of writhing cable tentacles.

The Operator sits on a raised stool before an intricate control panel. The Operator's clothes covered with a residue of white dust.

A robotic arm flies out from the hatch. It holds a tiny pointed hat from which hangs an excessively large visor. The machine tries to place the conical hat on the Operator's head.

The arm tentatively extends, hesitates, then retreats back into its hole.

The hatch closes, revealing the reflection of the apprehensive Operator. The drawn smile now smudged away.

An old boneshaker of a bicycle is chained to the radiator on the far wall, locked with a shiny new chain and heavy brass padlock. The back wheel revolves slowly, carving a groove in the chalky floor.

The wheel runs an old dynamo which powers the back light. It glows, pulsing with a dim red light. A rich ruby heartbeat in the dismal chamber.

A bellows descends from above the machine. In panic the Operator grasps the bellows and clumsily forces the nozzle into a sphincter-like orifice in the machine. The Operator averts their face and squeezes the bellows. The room fills with a choking cloud of fine white dust.

The Monitor pops up out of the dust.

Physically taller than the Operator, the Monitor moves, as if on rusting wheels, in awkward jerks, reminiscent of a malfunctioning shopping trolley. Although clearly human, the Monitor's faceless movements are infused with the dance of machine motion. In one hand, the Monitor holds a clipboard.

The Monitor is dressed in a black boiler-suit. Painted on to the back of his apparel is an image of technologically modified human hands in a circular chain.

The Monitor examines a level indicator. Takes a device from a utility pouch. He points it at the Operator. It makes a quacking sound. The closer the device gets to the Operator, the louder and more urgent the quacks.

The Operator scowls at the Monitor. Then looks sheepishly at the control panel.

The Monitor makes a mark on the clipboard. White paper. White pen. White ink.

Fibreoptic lights bristle as the machine spasms. It emits a thunderous belch.

The Monitor vanishes like a popped balloon, leaving behind a cloud of shredded paper which falls to the floor. These tendrils clog the machine, hampering its movements. The Operator brushes this detritus aside.

The Operator bushes the paper strands from his body. Some of it remains on their head.

The Operator cagily eyes the machine. A white face reflected in the hatch. The Operator's eyes are drawn to the "off switch". An immense red mushroom. A clown's nose. A tremendous red boil on the rump of the machine.

The Operator sharply turns to face the bicycle, a desire to escape painted across his face.

The bicycle wheel spins faster now. Its light glows brighter.

The image of the door clearly only painted on the wall.

The Operator decisively takes a key from a trouser pocket.

With an owl screech the hatch is suddenly open again.

The Operator fumbles and drops the key. It sparkles in the

darkness beneath the machine. Just out of reach.

The Operator anxiously readies himself for the hat.

Nothing emerges. The hatch shuts again.

The Operator panics and kicks the machine. There is a hollow gasp. All lights die, throwing the room into total darkness. The machine gurgles violently in a death rattle.

The dim red light of the bicycle is reflected in the terror of the Operator's stricken eyes.

Fizzing spasmodically, the ceiling lights endeavour to re-ignite. The spasms grow intense and stroboscopic.

A subaquean luminescence as the machine's fibreoptic hairs bristle in unison.

The room glows. Its light building till it is strong and steady. The machine inhales, sucking all the dust from the room.

The hatch flies open.

The tiny hat shoots out of the hatch, landing on his head with a sickening bang.

With a drunken monkey motion, the Operator grabs the air for the absent bellows. Finally, the bellows fall from the ceiling, shrunken and exhausted. The Operator uses the sight attached to the visor to insert the bellows into the machine's sphincter, with precision.

He operates the bellows. Nothing happens. The equipment tries to shoot back into the hatch but fails. A terrible grinding noise as the Operator tries to prevent this. There is a struggle. A noise of breaking wheels on a runaway train that emits from the body of the machine. The hat will not retract. The robot arm falls limp. The Operator screws up his face at the stench of burning.

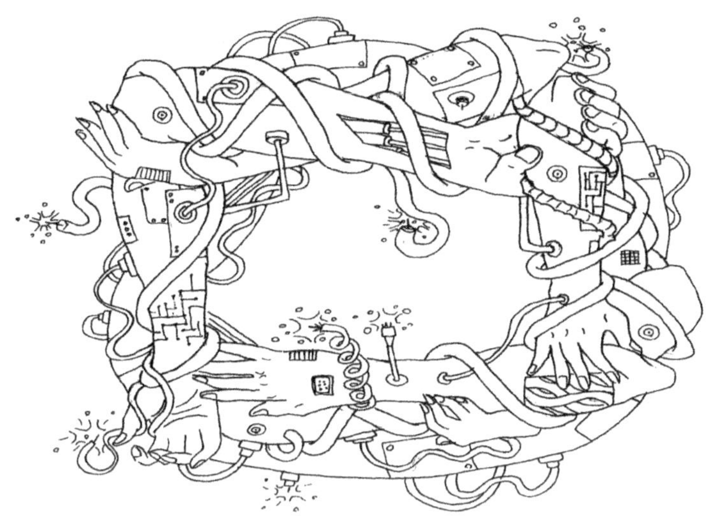

The furtive Operator swiftly drops to the floor. He endeavours to retrieve the sparkling keys, scrabbling under the hot machine. The Operator wipes sweat from his eyes, unaware of a black slime on his hands. Black panda marks cover each eye.

Just as the Operator's fingers close on the keys, The Monitor appears. The Operator panics at the sound of quacking. He quickly hides the keys. The Operator slides out from under the machine. As he does so, the machine seems to maliciously grab the Operator's hair and coats it with green goo.

Under the Monitor's blank gaze, the Operator pathetically attempts to flatten down the greasy meringues of his now green hair. The Monitor blankly prods the Operator with a long, thin sink plunger, forcing The Operator back into the chair. The Operator pushes the machine's broken arm violently out of his way.

The Operator grimaces in pain.

The Monitor efficiently produces an almost microscopic

screwdriver. A jewel glint. In the other hand, the Monitor holds a massive Victorian oil can. An elaborate microscope-like contraption telescopes from the Monitor's eye. The Monitor leans over the wounded bellows. The Monitor works back along the body of the machine with the screwdriver and flips back the carapace to reveal the runny organs of its interior. The Monitor pushes into the gooey body of the machine – swimming through the fluid guts within until their body is almost entirely absorbed.

The Bicycle.

The distant sounds of a circus.

The Operator's scalp unpeels. The top of his skull raises and expands like a bone umbrella to reveal a circus tent – bright reds and yellows in stark contrast to the dreary grey room. The squeals of children, the roll of drums, amazed gasps, rapturous applause, the incessant barp-barping of a clown-car hooter comes from inside the big top tent, where a clown emerges onto the sawdust of the ring. It is clearly the Operator. The massive clown sits on a miniature unicycle. There is only one tiny child in the audience. It is the Monitor. The delighted clown cycles freely, careering around the dark ring. The clown holds a bucket. The clown sails past the child on the cycle. Once. Twice. Lost in the dark as he cycles away. Then he looms out of the darkness, heading straight for the child, the bucket held before him like a weapon. He makes a motion to throw the bucket over the child.

CLOWN

Shall I?

Suddenly the machine coughs and splutters, then bursts into life. The bellows whip back into the ceiling. The power dies with an ear-piercing Doppler whine.

The cranial parasol above The Operator's skull snaps shut and the scalp zips up in an instant.

The painted door.

The Operator grabs the bicycle, removes the lock and chain. The bike struggles to escape his grasp.

The Operator wheels the bike out into the centre of the room. The handlebars come off. They hang pathetically in the Operator's hands. As the bicycle tries to escape, the Operator tries to reattach the handlebars. He manages to fix the handlebars back on. The Operator sits on the bike. The rear light dims as the bike is brought to heel.

The bike rears up suddenly, its front wheel comes off and spins away. The Operator lurches forward and smacks nose first into the handlebars. They detach again. Peddling frantically The Operator manages to stay mounted. He lurches about on the back wheel of the bicycle.

The terrified Operator battles to control this makeshift clumsy unicycle. It sails pell-mell around the room, like an untamed steed. The Operator throws the handlebars away. The rear light glows blood red with anger.

Abruptly, the Operator is sent tumbling through the air. He collapses on the floor with a horrendous and sickening crash.

The Operator looks up from the floor at the painted door.

The Bicycle dies. The back wheel stops. The red light slowly extinguishes.

Blood leaks from the Operator's nose. Black panda eyes, shiny red nose, greasy black and green hair perched on his scalp. The Operator now the clown he dreams of becoming.

The Operator struggles to his feet. The Monitor extracts themself from within the machine and it explodes into life.

The Operator hastily takes his place back at the controls. The hat and visor, with the sight attached, slams onto his head. Lights flash. The machine heaves. Bloody and confused, the Operator frantically taps away on the control buttons.

The machine rumbles obscenely. Three tubes twist out over its body and meet in a single nipple-like nozzle.

An empty glass vial, no bigger than a thimble, comes out of the body of the machine. The vial hovers on a jet of air beneath the nozzle.

Buffeted by the now shuddering machine, the Operator attempts to keep the sight located on the nozzle and the vial.

The tubes twist frantically. The machine heaves. The Operator taps at the console. With an urgent thunder, the machine emits gaseous multicoloured farts. The Operator's chair bucks like a rodeo horse.

In orgasmic urgency, the machine heaves. Intense pressure within causes it to steam. Just as it seems the machine will explode, a single tiny drop of condensed summer blue-sky eases from the nozzle in ultra slow mo. The thick liquid topaz takes an eternity to fall into the waiting glass vial.

Its exertions over, the machine sighs with exhaustion, rolls over and goes to sleep.

Exquisite blue liquid in the tiny glass vial.

Captivated by beauty, the Operator's face looms closer. He winces at the stench.

A hatch in the machine opens revealing asbestos gloves, goggles and tongs. The Operator takes the gloves, then the goggles, and puts all these items on. He picks up the tongs and grasps the vial.

The Monitor winds a creaky wheel. A rusty birdcage rises into the room from a circular hole in the floor. The Operator squeezes into this miniature lift. He struggles to keep the smelly vial upright, and as far away from his nose as the tiny space will allow. The Monitor winds the wheel. The lift ascends.

The Operator steps out of the cage and climbs the long winding stair. These stairs hug and circle around the exterior cast-iron body of a colossal structure, somewhat like a Victorian gasometer. The Operator climbs and climbs.

The Operator climbs.

He reaches the top of this enormous metal vat. He leans over the rim. Beneath the Operator is a vast lake of liquid sky.

With great care and precision, the Operator tips the tiny vial. The drop of summer topaz falls into the lake of blue below.

A slow mo crown of droplets forms and falls. Ripples echo away to the distant shores of the tank.

The Operator pauses for a moment. Bliss brings a clown-sized smile to his sad face. The Operator cranes his neck and looks around over the lip of the gasometer, and the endless uncountable gasometers beyond it, and stares up at the continual steel sky of the never-ending warehouse that houses them all.

A tear forms in his eye. It runs down his cheek and drops into the metal vat.

A slow mo crown of droplets forms and falls. Ripples echo away to the distant shores of the tank.

The Operator stows equipment, then descends the stair once more.

TALKSFOOLS

"out of a blurred horizon between a blank and anonymous plane and a cruel and vacant sky comes a small dark spot. it grows. an ink blot on foolscap, expanding into some kind of figure. we perceive as a crossing more fully over into the borderline of our perceptions that, as with we too, there is a bowler hat and tatty ill-fitting clothes, that are made up of patches, patches that are tiny, and individual, fragments of pure colour in an otherwise empty world. we waddles towards us, seemingly content in two dimensions, or should that be dementions? we grows rapidly from the size of a dwarf, until we stands in front of us fully grown. we bows. looks drunk. so we does. the motley skin has a green tint. arh yes! yet more colour we brings us! the nose is hideously and hilariously red. we can see. apparently, we likes a tipple. old devil. so where does we end? not sure. a sad mouth fixed in an uncontrollable grin. we stands before us, slightly contorted and lightly murmurs words we do not rightly understand. they may be ours. perhaps it is because we cannot hear them, that we have difficulty. if we take the fingers out of the ears, who knows what will leak out? we lost a brain that way, and gained the birds. should have kept the fingers in. shut up! how many of us are there? we looks at the bottle despairingly and we see in front of us a kaleidoscope of bottles, each reflecting us. we seem to have been drinking too. incorrigible! encouraging! we all like a drop, don't we? a fall, a slip, a plummet. back to the point-of-view. if there is a point to the view. we may be wrong. at least a view corresponding to the one previous to the one we've just had, we see the bottle thrown away and we waddle off past us, to shrink back down to the size of a dwarf, or child, and then finally become only a blip on the frontier between black and white, and then, and then, gone. but we do not see we do so, so we can only guess about it. our world remains the first blurred horizon and the first blank and anonymous plane, as we are not prepared to move and follow. the others, the hypothetical ones, we can only speculate upon and their similarity to the blank and anonymous plane, with which we are familiar, is perhaps, not so assured. at first glance, we would have said we was us anyway, wouldn't' we? if we haven't said far too much already. we have. we blabbed. we babbled. in which case it doesn't matter. well said! we was certainly very similar. no we wasn't! yes we was! well we've forgotten what we were talking about. yes that's just like us. no it's not. yes it is. no it's not. oh alright, have it our way. we don't want it our way, we want it our way and that's the end of the matter. oh, we give up! that's just like us. presumably it is known, if we did vanish into this other, as yet hypothetical, horizon, we'll never get our nose back because we had it you know. what? our nose, we had our nose, it was exactly the same. well if we did vanish into this horizon, or presumably if we does so, all we have to do is wait here until we pops out the other side and appears on the blurred horizon in front of us and we'll get the nose back. good thinking, we is a clod. let's just wait here then. fancy a drink? where did you get it? it was left behind. we'd better hope we comes back too. why? we had our clothes, those clothes were exactly the same as ours. really? yes. the same patches of colour. just like these. yes the very same. well we never. well, we never what? well we're never in the never-never. but we's got the clothes. yes, we see, perhaps we should just drop it. drop what? this bomb we've got in the pocket. give it here let us look. no, it's ours and as we could be standing behind us, it is best, as we certainly don't propose to turn around and look at any other plane – anonymous or otherwise – this one, this plane is the one for us, in view of the state of affairs we propose to blow up everything behind us, before we gets the hands on this bomb. yes, we can see the attraction in it, it is certainly an appealing plan and it certainly is a very nice bomb. can we help in any way? yes, now just hold this bomb a second. let go. we can't let go. let go. no. let go! we're fed up of trying. let go first. we can't. neither can we. may we be of assistance? yes, where did we spring from? we came up from behind. oh we did, did we? yes. well here, hold this bomb. thank you, we should be glad to. don't give it. why not? because we have to blow it up. we stole our nose. we did, did we? light the bomb! the lighting of the bomb is not a job for the likes of us. but we stole our clothes. we did, did we? yes. this certainly is a very nice bomb. who asked for an opinion? good question. do we have a light? yes, we do, somewhere. shit! it's happened again. what has? the hand, we can't get it out of the pocket. neither can we. perhaps if we pull with the free arms, we can get them out. we can try. we certainly can. what shall we do with this bomb? whatever we like, put it in the pocket if we want. but it's too big. it went into the pocket. it never did. we'll prove it. give us the bomb. there see, it fits. there's room for us in there too. we bet there isn't. shouldn't be so hasty, they are big pockets. okay, we'll climb in then. be our guest, come on put a foot in, here goes nothing. we shouldn't be so sure. from nothing nothing comes, but nothing never goes. never? arrr! what happened? we fell in! did we have the bomb? we're not sure, we'll check. well have we got the bomb, or what? yes, the bomb is in there and quite safe, probably. better put it in another pocket so that we can't get a hand on it. good idea. what's the matter? nothing. not that again. there is a lot of it about. well, we think even though we is in the pocket, we think we should still blow up the behind us. why? just to be sure. we don't want any more of this turning up malarkey. no, we're not wrong there, we was a nuisance. yes. where was we from? ask. good idea, help us in. better go via the other pocket. why? it's best to be safe. that's right. as long as we know, don't wait the pockets connect. we are sure of it. we are? it is inevitable. inevitable? yes, we'll say hello and make enquires as to personal history. Yes, we would be grateful if we did so and if we find a piano. yes, we'll let us knoooooooooow! what was that? we didn't catch it. we all like a drop. ho-hum, goodbye as well, hope we find a piano in there. we'd better ponder on where the nose has gone. we need a drink. goes without saying. it was silent? silent. talk's cheap. yes, and words are empty. out of nothing, the nothing comes, then goes without saying. don't speak of it, or we'll make it happen. we already did. suppose we are next to nothing. the saying makes it so. but the words are empty. is that why the talk is so cheap.

now we are next to nothing there is nothing for it but to come to nothing. perhaps we should move as a precaution? best not to look back. we wouldn't want to see nothing. we perhaps should walk forwards, towards the margin. the nose might be there. the bottle is in the hand. lucky it was left behind. here's to us. yes let's put it all in the behind us. yes, lets. do you suppose we will shrink? oh, it's the silent treatment, is it? the pocket is soundproofed perhaps? the legs move themselves. how fortunate. the shrinking is worrying. When we are a blip, will it hurt us? the shrinking certainly is a worry and us without a piano. it only we had the piano. wonder if we are the dwarf yet, or the child. probably. we've probably told the story of the king who had a dwarfing box? well why not tell it again? well why not? because it tells us. well, let it. there was this king, he collected oddities and unusual human specimens and allowed them free reign over his kingdom, which may have been a blank and anonymous plane like this one, or it may have been of the kind that we have designated hypothetical. have a drink, don't mind if we do. we don't? if we could remember it we might not want to hear it again. We are made smaller by the lost piano. we are? yes. did we create us? good question. we may as well forget the king. we may as well. we may as well what? continue. the legs move themselves. true enough. where are we going? we are trying not to lose face. we do seem to have misplaced parts of it. it's a worry. it was trying to keep the nose clean that did it. it was hard keeping it to the grindstone. it wouldn't come clean. where is the grindstone now? it is in the pocket perhaps? Of course, the inevitability of it. of course, it changes everything. it does? we would have thought that we would have thought that we would bet we might be different. if we were we would not be the same now

that everything has changed. break the heart for we must hold
the tongue. yes, we had best change the subject the tongue
might become loose. we object, we haven't tried knocking sense
into it. break it and have done with it. holding the tongue tastes
nasty. the heart is broken already and we know it. shattered. we
would have it horsewhipped but we haven't got a horse. that's
what broke it, the absence of the nose, and the piano and the
grindstone and now the missing horse. it's all too much. it might
be of some conciliation to us that there may be a horse in the
pocket. the place where fresh is the taste. is that so? we know it,
we were told. we was. the taste is fresh. we was nosey when we
had a nose, always sticking it in with the oar. those were the days.
perhaps we's got the oar stashed with the nose. we didn't see an
oar on the face. we's crafty. we may have had the wool pulled over
the eyes. how else did we get away with the nose? how else? we
should have stayed put. we rushed in again. we were soon parted.
we should just stay where we were. in the middle of nowhere.
alright. there's one born every minute. what's born every minute?
one. oh, what's that then? we are not sure. how long is a minute
then? oh, about a quarter of a mile. oh, is it snowing? it's hard to
tell. it could have been snowing. it could still be snowing. if only
we could find the piano. the legs move themselves. the piano
has no legs. were the legs stolen? a legless piano. a tragedy,
it hasn't got over it yet. it drinks to forget? less dangerous than
forgetting to drink. have we tried both? we don't recall. if we can't
remember then we must be drunk. then how come we've still got
the legs? yes, but they move themselves. we must stage a coup.
where do we get a stage from? when we are born, we cry for we
are come to this great stage. are we the ones who are born every
minute then. if so why aren't we crying? well the doesn't appear

to be a stage, at this stage, oh, curiouser and curiouser, about
that coup. we must put a foot down. we don't want to be out on a
limb any more. we want our legs back. perhaps we should find the
piano's legs first. is it very unhappy in the pocket? very unhappy.
there's a bomb in there. we know. it won't do anything rash, will
it? it may even use the grindstone in a way that might have tragic
consequences. why did we ever get involved with a piano in the
first place. don't we think we've gone on long enough? brevity's
the soul of wit. we that has a little tiny wit with a hey ho the wind
and the rain must make content with fortune's fit, though the rain
it raineth every day. and the snow too? more than likely. it's hard
to tell. we'd be content with a fortune, we wouldn't care if it fit or
not. well the face doesn't. why should anything else? if we'd been
more careful with the nose, since we lost the nose the whole
face must have worked its way loose. beaten by the nose again.
we are in serious danger of losing the face. it's a constant effort.
we need a screw to help us reattach ourselves. before the face
goes the same way as the piano. legless with a number of screws
missing. this prophecy merlin shall make. what's a merlin? a bird
or a brain? we're not sure. if we were to swap a bird for a brain
would we be worse off? but we suppose that we must consider
the role of the bird in all this. we would need a brain first anyway.
why don't we get this merlin to make us a brain? we have already
determined that merlin makes things. we have? prophesies. but
that doesn't mean that merlin can get us a brain. why don't we just
use the bird for a brain? we've heard it can be done. in our case
we've probably had a whole flock of foul fowl nesting in the belfry.
we certainly have and that merlin as well. that's why the fingers
are placed in the ears, to keep everything in. they certainly are.
another fine mess we got ourselves out of. now we understand.

how do we hear? we hear through the fingers. they are very sensitive to sound. give it a rest. and how do we give a rest? we try our best under difficult circumstances. these are trying times. we are not wrong. we've been tried and tested and approved by the manufacture. we have? yes. was that in the place where fresh is the taste? inevitably. we felt sure. it was a dead giveaway. that doesn't sound very nice. we are not a charity. best to kill anything you give away first. charity begins at home. it is where the heart is. but we don't know where the heart is and it's broken anyway. by the absence? by the absence. the nose, the piano, the legs, the grindstone, the missing screws, merlin, the brain, the birds. the absence shattered the heart. so we have no home then. it's wherever the fragments of it are. so that's where charity can begin? we don't know we are not a charity. we must follow the nose where it leads. the heart may have attacked us anyway. that is a probability. if it had hardened up it may not have broken. that was its decision. wonder if we made enquiries as to personal history? perhaps we should go in and find out. it should be possible if we bend in the head. let's give it a try. here goes nothing. where? where what? where goes nothing? here. we better watch out then. we'd be safer in the pocket before the nothing comes. better hurry up then. what was that? nothing. we were too late then. apparently so. well better late than never. how can we be so sure? we have a bomb at least. we would be safer if we were with the bomb. it should be possible if we bend the head in. here goes nothing."

JUST FIVE MINUTES

(Written in partnership with AMBER LINELL)

A LIFT IN A BLOCK OF FLATS.
Looking down from a service hatch into the metal box of this movable room.

A lone dog is running restlessly around, frustrated. The lift makes a periodical ringing noise, as someone calls for the lift that does not move. When the bell rings, the dog stops running and sits.

NIGHT. A LIVING ROOM IN A BLOCK OF FLATS.
The sound of a TV gameshow. No one is watching.

The gigantic face of a mechanical baby doll coming closer and closer, jerking towards us. The toy walks forwards relentlessly with robotic determination. Increasingly the doll's movements become erratic as its mechanism winds down. It makes an electronic pinging sound similar to the ringing in the lift.

The clockwork runs out, leaving the doll caught frozen in mid-motion, holding itself in an unlikely posture on the floor of the living room.

The doll is snatched up by a young girl, MAXINE, who is about six years of age. She begins walking with the toy towards the window. Her mother calls her from outside the room.

MUM

Max! Bed in five minutes more, love.

Maxine looks at the doll.

MAXINE

Okay, Mum!

The girl opens the ajar window, and holds the doll out in the air, suspended by its hair.

The distant floor beneath the window from the doll's point of view.

The doll swings as Maxine talks to her. Then throws her up slightly and catches her.

MAXINE

Just five minutes more till mummy saves you!
And you'll be safe in bed. Just say your prayers.

Maxine moves the dolls hands together.

MAXINE

Go on, pray! Pray to be saved!

Maxine gets bored, slides down wall, ignores the TV as she picks up a book and becomes engrossed in it. The doll is abandoned at her feet next to crayons, colouring-in books and other stuff she has discarded.

Reflected in the window, the sparks of a firework going off outside.

LIFT. BLOCK OF FLATS.
Looking down from a service hatch on the dog in the lift. It is jumping up and around in sheer frustration.

NIGHT. ANOTHER LIVING ROOM IN A DIFFERENT FLAT IN THE SAME BLOCK.
The flat is similar to the other flat, but decorated very differently. The muted sounds of a party next door.

Looming towards us through steam comes the face of a young teenage boy. Eyes squinting. A look of distaste upon his somber face.

We see the boy's trainers as he sits at a table. He is sitting with his head over a bowl. A towel covering his head. There is a hand on top of his head forcing him to stay under.

A goldfish swimming around in a bowl. A male voice. It seems like it might be the fish talking, but it is the dad.

DAD

Er... What was I thinking?

There was something I'd forgotten.

A hand rubs his head robotically. The same person who is holding
the boy over the bowl, gesticulating and trying to remember. He
moves off towards a closed door that leads to a kitchen.

SON

Can I come out now?

DAD

Err. Hold on. Just wait. It's for your own good.

SON

Dad!

The phone rings before the man can get to the door. He stops
and answers it. He stands by the fish. As he stands talking, he
absentmindedly feeds the fish.

DAD

Oh hi. Sorry, I've been wracking my brains about something.
You've just reminded me, it's you that I should have rung.
Nah. I know how long your five minutes turn out to be.

The teenager moves to get up. Flakes of multi coloured fish-food
fall into the water. The teenager sits back down.

DAD

Stop fidgeting! No, Gill, not you. (laughs)
Yeah, that's right, he's sick.
I'm experimenting on him. Vic and hot water,
always clears the tubes. (laughs)

Yes, that's right.
No, I haven't had a cold for ages.

The boy's face looming through steam. Not listening to his father's conversation, the sounds of which are muted, or played backwards. A voice chatters meaninglessly. The son is concentrating on the music coming through the wall, from the party next door, which now seems louder and bassier.

From a crack in the kitchen door. The dad notices a whiff of steam. Wraps up his conversation, then goes to investigate.

DAD

What's that?
No, not you. Look, Gill, I've got to go.
I'll call you back later.

The father opens the kitchen door, then steam floods into the living room. An electric kettle has malfunctioned and is pumping large quantities of steam out. The steam rolls into and fills up the living room, surrounding the youth who remains unaware. The sounds of the father unplugging the kettle, then opening the kitchen window.

DAD

Don't just sit there. The kettle's knackered again. Open a window!

The teenager comes up from underneath the towel into a room full of steam. He instantly begins coughing horrendously.

LIFT BLOCK OF FLATS.

Looking down from a service hatch. The dog in the lift. This time it is just lying down and sleeping. Tired out.

NIGHT. OUT ON THE ROOF OF THE BLOCK OF FLATS.

The face of a sleeping drunken man, HARRY, wearing a party hat. Whispering and the distant noise of a party, playing the same record earlier coming through the walls. There is giggling, shushing and noise of clambering as a couple makes their way across the roof.

A slightly drunk male, DAN, and a female, LEO, of about 50 years of age stand over the sleeping man. The man has a firework rocket in his hand.

DAN

How did he get up here?

LEO

Same way as us. (both laugh)

The man walks off with the rocket and begins to set it up, while the woman sits down next to the sleeping man and tries to wake him up. Harry opens his eyes.

LEO

Playing gooseberry again, Harry?

HARRY

Wha...?

DAN (Shouting)

*I went all the way to Kimbolton to get this rocket and it was sold
to me by a priest.*

LEO

Er?

(laughing)

Dan pulls out a cigarette lighter, lights the rocket's fuse. Dan
steps back.

LEO

Happy anniversary!

HARRY and LEO

5, 4, 3, 2, 1.

(Together, yet slightly out of sync.)

The fuse burns down to the end. Nothing happens. It seems to
be a dud. The rocket stays where it is.
Harry begins to stand up. But is pushed back down by Leo.

HARRY

I'll sort it.

LEO

No you bloody won't!

Just wait 5 minutes they always go off in the end!

Dan Joins Harry and Leo. Harry continues to try to get up and

Leo gently stops him.

DAN

What anniversary?

LEO

We've known each other 100 days!

DAN

Really!

LEO

Well, more or less. (Both laugh).

Dan and Leo kiss. They do not notice that drunk Harry is crawling off towards the rocket.

DAN

Sorry about the rocket, I can never get them up when I'm drunk.
(Both giggle).

Leo and Dan kiss again. Dan is crawling near the rocket, then begins to stagger to his feet.

The rocket.

Harry is on his feet, trying to light a Zippo lighter, still about 10 feet from the rocket. The torch of the lighter burning in his hand. He staggers towards the firework, lighter outstretched.

The rocket.

Dan and Leo stop snogging, then notice that Harry isn't there. And rush after him to stop him. But he is too close, they hesitate.

LEO

Stop!

DAN

No!

Harry frozen in front of the rocket. Dan and Leo way behind.

INT. OUTSIDE THE ENTRANCE TO THE LIFT, BLOCK OF FLATS.

With a tremendous juddering, the doors open. Revealing the dark interior of the lift. The sound of a rocket going off. The dog, who remains in the lift, stares out looking from side to side.

The sound of an explosion, followed by laughter from up on the roof.

SKOO

ri-mari, wi goo atz urdz, tri fu stand. wi sten to ri-mari az shim goo tru skoo. wi ere. shim lurn, wi lurn. wi tri sez urdz fu ri-mari. wi tri splane.

wi ol ol skoo. wi lodge firm onz olitary taintop, fullimatik. dredz ov yeeer pass. nuwhen croz salt wet-her ta reach uz. dredz nd dredz ov yeeer turn ta sandz nd haps illionz pass.

onz our land iz nuwhen bu uz. wi run, bu empti. nuwhen cum. nubother. wi fullimatik. wi fix. wi clean. wi gleam. dam nd sun nd wind duce nergi inuz.

wi readi.

den atz las small boat croz. den nother. nd slow, folk swell ere neath uz. till ventual noo illage cum to tainfoot, nd folk turn turf nd sow full wiv crops az far az wi can peer. wi watch az illage grow nd grow.

den atz las, brave wunz skale midable ight to vestigate uz

onz our peak, out findz our oose. wi kill fust vaders az zay temp smash inz. nex vaders openuz up right way, wi kill allz bu wun, az zay tempt sneak out thu kave, rongway. zey sorbed fu-evs, az bone brave nd blud brave, once not wi, now makebrave wallz nd hallz nd allz ov skoo fu-evs.

den las wun gez wi, atz las. ri-mari inz joinz. liv side wi az ogrammed. liv inz uz, no tempt scape. ri-mari. fust. wi feed nd care nd skoo fust wun till yeeer onz ri-mari pass allz tess nd gez ventual tonomi. leesed.

ri-mari, skoo iz ducate place max imumsec. fullimatic.

so goo ri-mari, goo tainfoot illage nd etch uz rong-unz. wi lurn um, az inz pass. wi take aptiv int wi fu gud, less zey lurn, if um gez tru skoo's n-term, zen wi urn um oose.

NINTH LIFE

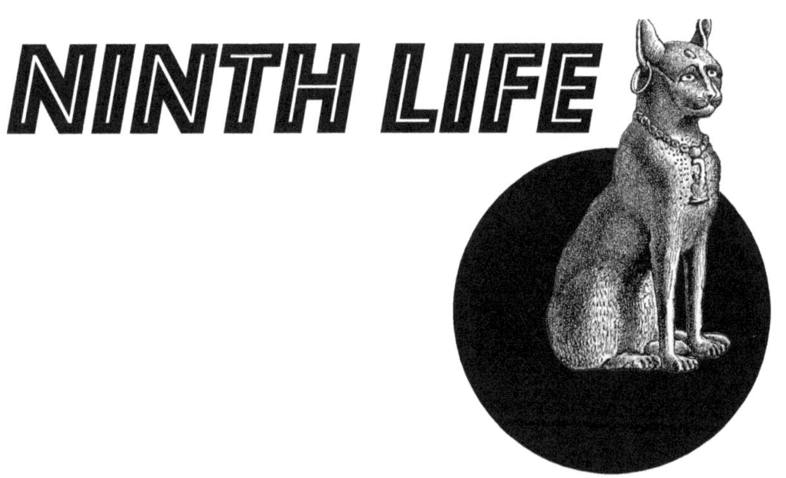

Sextus's obsession with being devoured alive by a big cat may well have been realised. This thought grew in me. Haunting my mind for nine months, my certainty swelling as each day passed. No tracks of him after Tuesday July 19th 2022. At the height of the heatwave he evaporated. After this date I could find no further trace of him or the panther which consumed his waking thought, if not his body. That is, until now.

Though his van was found burnt out at Northampton's crumbling concrete edge, there was no sign of any remains within its metallic entrails. Sweating police prodded at it briefly. Their probing half-hearted pussyfooting, toying with before abandoning the scorched chassis to the Council's whim. Local Authority hi-viz agents swiftly removed the prize of the decorated carcass before I could add it to my collection; although I have rescued some digital images of it, helpfully recorded by the constables. A little money, in the right hands, you understand, works wonders. Unfortunately, the photographs do not capture all of the iconic designs and arcane sigils that coated his snuffed vehicle. The Transit's terminal location remains as mysterious as its owner's. So far I have been unable to bring the trophy of its corpse to join my collection of his garage doors in their isolated security out here at The Stables. Mental health issues, rather than foul play, Old Bill's conclusion. An ill blast-furnace wind melting short their investigation, everyone was going bloody mad in the heat. Still, there was the problem of the lack of a body, living or otherwise. But their interest was neutered, lacking real concern, one less fluffy nut-job. Though, if he is truly dead, he seems not to have lost his artistic abilities.

Sextus Shaman, formerly Tom Bartholomew, had left a vivid trail for me to follow. An indelible psychedelic scent sprayed in gorgeous and potentially lucrative graff, around much of the centre of urine stained Blighty. At the skeleton of his dead van, his path seemingly ended as abruptly as one of his explosive rages. Since his disappearance I have followed his steps to many dilapidated ammonia perfumed locations, filled with similar offerings of generic British detritus: endless abandoned plastic, noz canisters tainted with rust, crumpled beer cans, dog-ends and totemic black bags of mutt-shit hung from bushes to ward off God knows what. It was in such marginal places around the Midlands that I located the succession of eight vivid renderings of his iconic Panthera pardus, and began my negotiations. To me the order of the images seemed to reveal a visionary progression of deep import. I had Kitty and Giacomo my technicians fly in to supervise their safe collection and installation. They worked with a small crew of hand-picked specialists all of whom we could trust. They were the only ones who had any inkling of what I had gathered out here at The Stables. Since they have left the country, I am on my own to enjoy them.

I have more than a dozen properties around the world, but The Stables is one of the more obscure. Ostensibly owned by a shell company, it is reasonably isolated and I store a small but not insignificant part of my collection here. The security systems are state of the art. Every so often I feel the need to be on my own, and The Stables is where I withdraw to. Sooner or later I would reveal the mysteries of what I had hunted down to other private retinas, and then possibly a brief release to public scrutiny, before trading the works for a significant return. Not any time soon though. The images haunted me. I had to have them all in my paws. His entire oeuvre was as significant as Louis Wain or Jean-Michel Basquiat and just as worthy of investment, and I could have most of them for a squeal. Easy meat, when your talons are made of money. The enormous magical moggies were just the start. I wanted everything he created.

Every example of this extraordinary panther cycle proved to be proximal to potential sightings of large non-native felidae. All of which had been reported on the website Feral. Dates of production helpfully woven into his distinctive feline unguis tag. Like the one I discovered on our bullet-proof gate here at The Stables just a few hours ago. I have been inside ever since. It doesn't feel safe out there. High-tech kit is all very well, but I am starting to regret not having my security team at hand.

The new image on the doors is the first of his works that I have in my possession that has not cost me anything, so far. Clearly, the ninth and possibly the terminal creation in the enneadic sequence; this new work a gestalt of nine images of panthers that echoed and recalled the previous works, though in a slightly different order. It was reminiscent of a comic book page. It suggests multiple journeys to and from an underworld of sorts, katabasis followed by anabasis. It is a series of triumphal cat comebacks from the world of death; each return to life marked by a successful kill. This is alluded to in the blood-coated fur of the final animal, stained as it is in darkening claret which looks too real.

This new work is much simpler in its draftsmanship than his previous work, possibly due to haste in its construction. It displays an urgent development in style, moving towards radical simplicity, almost like a late Matisse. So much fuss and bother burnt away by a visit to the abyss, perhaps. Yet I am certain that it shows the claw marks of the same artist. However, his previous images were complex vortices of fascinating, overpowering and horrifically extreme detail, reminiscent of Richard Dadd's oils. Though epically large, typically filling his preferred canvas of two or three garage doors, they contained a similar hypnotic and claustrophobic power to the paintings of the Victorian lunatic and murderer, and it was that ravenous attention that partly drew me to them. The works were not so much composed, but explosions of disconnected elements; amputated body parts, disembodied eyes, creepy crawlies, CCTV cameras and pyramids were common – inferno and flames everywhere. The rare human visages that could be found within the works were blank and asymmetrical, the right of the face as you looked at it characteristically shrunken in, or elongated. Bodies often appeared to be changing sex. Though the big cat's–heads that dominated the works were always implacably, unreadably symmetrical, terrifyingly so. There was often intrusion of text in the images and repeated, overworked meandering geometric enquires that zigzagged around the creations, reminiscent of waves of energy that seemed to have the power of disintegration beams or mind-controlling rays. What words that could be made out suggested the anguish of someone who finds himself adrift, an unrecognisable piece in a never ending procession of other objects.

And, on occasion, I noticed seemingly random quotations and references to the poem Jubilate Agno by Christopher Smart. A work, I have discovered, that obsessed him.

'For he is of the Tribe of Tiger'

'For the Cherub Cat is a term of the Angel Tiger'

'For I am a mouse. And the mouse is a creature of great personal valour.'

And sometimes the writing seemed to attempt a reversal of the pattern expressed in transubstantiation, in the summoning of a deity for the purpose of consuming him.

'Oh, Son of Man-eater, we are food for The Lord!'

'Sabre tooth Jesus, come for us!'

Frank James, the anomalous big cat enthusiast and owner of the Feral website, agreed to meet me inside St Matthew's in Northampton, the largest church in the vicinity and site of one of Sextus's final recorded meetings. The dump of a town does not even have an Anglican cathedral or much else really. The closest they have to one is this late 19th Century ego-trip, in the area known as Phippsville. Viewed from the back, with its towers, spires and pointed roof. it looked almost like a rough realisation of a Germanic faeryland; had not the whole apparently ancient edifice been instantly made clearly fake by dint of it growing out of a modest lawn, and by being constructed of a kind of cheese, in hand-hewn bricks of a yellow-brown material that passed for stone in this part of the world. I didn't like the place. Necessary evils, visiting the church and the town; they had things I needed, but nevertheless I wanted to get back to The Stables as quickly as possible. I see now that this was a mistake and must have been where my trail was picked up.

The climax of the original sequence of eight, I discovered a block away from the church. Until earlier today, I believed it to be the last example of his work. Though the nominal owner of the garage proved more recalcitrant than the others, I was eventually able to deal with him. The masterpiece was originally located in a cobbled alleyway in sight of St Matthew's. An enormous metallic image rendered with genius, it filled the front of a relatively new double-garage. The melanistic phantom carnivore seemingly guarded by brutalistic cartoon tumescences, rendered in various colour marker-pens by numerous anonymous piss-artists; these stubby deformities standing comic sentry on the adjacent decaying doors while the anomalous big cat, ablaze, stared upwards. The taut form detonating out of a flat background nebular of stars and tiny insects; ants and aphids, bees and beetles, cockroaches and cootie, fleas and flies, mites and mosquitoes, termites and ticks. Each bug's depiction fastidiously accurate, each rendered sun a cold and distant eye burning in an alien, two dimensional way, as though it hated the third dimension and wanted to make the whole of everything flat. Locking its vision onto its prey, the church's spire, the predator's stance signalled it was about to pounce and rip the throat out of a rival god. I arranged to remove the doors with the penises on too, even though they were not by Sextus. I thought they would add a tragic quality to the installation I had planned.

Yes, a vicar at St Matthew's had commissioned a Henry Moore and Graham Sutherland for the church back in the '40s. Both artists overrated. However, it was not these grafters on the visual plane that made the place significant to Sextus. No, its attraction was in the fact that it was the sonic birthplace of Britten's Rejoice in the Lamb, with its mad cat Jeoffry words, hijacked from Smart's Jubilate Agno. This is what Frank James was to make apparent to me. Delighting in the fact of his privileged knowledge, and what he believed was the simple truth that he'd been in his presence and I never would be. St Matthew's was almost the last place he saw Sextus. One of the final recorded times that anyone glimpsed him, till perhaps now. The artist went there seeking transcendence in a live performance of the piece, on the site of its original emanation, and he had invited Frank along. I found Frank's claims to have enjoyed the performance a little difficult to believe. He was sleazy and repellent with a carnivorous glint. An individual obsessed with proving the truth of anomalous big cats, though with enough wily wit to turn his fanaticism for ABCs into a living of sorts. At our meeting he sported an item of his own merch, a Feral branded t-shirt, one with the legend, 'I am hunting for cougar'. This was slightly more tasteful than the reference to a big pussy gone wild, which he bragged was his best selling item, outselling anything by Sextus that he'd commissioned. He recounted his escapades with 'Sex', as he called him, following up reports of sightings across the Midlands that summer, with diligent searches for scat or paw prints. Somehow Sextus would always be in the vicinity first. Sometimes, even before the sighting had been posted on Feral. As Frank set up his motion-triggered infrared cameras, Sextus would appear.

Perhaps I have been spending too long alone. I never saw Sextus in the flesh, but the more I stare at the insubstantial monochrome image recorded by the CCTV that guards the gate, the more I can see a familiar spectral figure trying to resolve itself into this human dimension. Pareidolia, no doubt, but for all that it looks remarkably like the shape of a man carrying a can of spray-paint. And there's something else: predatory eyes. Eight pairs, picked out in the infrared of my CCTV, staring down at the property from up in the trees.

'FJ', as Sextus allegedly called him, and Frank insisted I call him, had come to my attention as one of the original champions of the artist's talent. Commissioning images for limited edition shirts that grew popular beyond the Fortean community they were initially aimed at, becoming de rigueur particularly with skaters. Eventually some of Sextus's images were even spotted on numerous rap stars and catwalks. Frank also commissioned a series of bronze pendants, cast precisely at an hour of great import in the season of Leo by a master smith in Pakistan. The times were calculated by electional astrological means. Following a precise series of instructions set out by Sextus to 'imbue them with phenomenal powers'. Frank definitely was a good salesman. These amulets were based on the Hohlentstien Löwenmensch, a blend of a cave lion and human, carved from mammoth ivory 40,000 years ago. It is the world's oldest known sculpture of an imaginary creature. Frank was insistent that Sextus would not take a bean from him for these works. That the money they brought in should be gifted to 'the poverty-stricken of the world'. I suspected that was a euphemism for Frank's bank account. I had recently deposited a grand into it, in order to secure the final example of Sextus's magical lion-man cast. Frank had brought it along in person to give to me. I have it in my hands now. It feels strangely warm and cold simultaneously. It's helping me focus on the CCTV and the security tech.

Frank explained that he sat through the rendition of the Cantata with a mixture of interest and fear. The look on Sextus's face haunted him. He'd gone 'somewhere else'. Sextus was temperamental at the best of times, but he feared if he raised the subject of making more works for Feral with him, he might kick off and rare up. It had happened to him before… once bitten… But he knew that this was perhaps his last chance before the artist's reputation grew too big for the likes of Feral. Frank need not have worried. At the end of the recitation, he leaned into him and said, 'I've had a few ideas for designs for you. I'll do them if I survive! "Let Nimrod, the mighty hunter, bind a leopard to the altar and consecrate his spear to the Lord." Know what I mean?' Frank did not know what he meant.

I am starting to wonder who Nimrod is here.

Later, as they sat together in the White Elephant, the closest pub to the church, Sextus carried on in a similar manner muttering about stalking… the cat was out of the bag… beast hunts beast… the great work is not for money… a predator was out there… they want to put them all in the circus… the Hohlentstien Löwenmensch is not only for protection… These utterances seemed to Frank to be paranoid ravings. Given his previous run-ins, Frank was cautious, hesitant to press the artist. Though he wished he had. He felt that with Sextus's disappearance his luck had dried up. Big cats seemed to have fled the island. No reports for weeks and weeks. Perhaps if he had helped the poor lad things might be different. I almost believed that Frank liked him. However, the recently deposited grand made me question that.

Before they parted for the final time, Sextus seemed to find focus. It may have been the treble single-malt kicking in. He monologued at Frank a detailed exposition of the 'ray cat solution', an idea to use genetic modification to create a breed of 'radiation cats', felines that change colour when they are in proximity to nuclear waste. Cats had lived closely with humans for thousands of years; it was supposed that this would continue into the deep future. For it to work it was necessary to breed the animals then spread the word of this concept deep into the mythological mind of humankind, so that fear and avoidance would be an immediate response to encountering one of these unprecedented fur-alarm beasts. The outcome in ten thousand years time, humans would be warned if they tried to build houses out of atomic materials or use them for currency. This sounded like more madness to Frank, but he looked into it later and it was a genuine plan. One created by brainiacs who were part of the Human Interference Task Force, at the Yucca Mountain Nuclear Waste Repository back in the 80s. Frank was planning on branching out and creating a line of products based on this concept that glow in the dark, t-shirts, mugs, jigsaws. He wished he had thought of that while he sat with Sextus.

The artist was animated; he did not believe this plan to modify cats would work as intended. For him, it needed to go further; the relationship must be with something that humans had had longer, much longer, than the concept of pets. The transformation of the cat must truly engender terror. There was a way. The Hohlentstien Löwenmensch provided the clue. I keep pondering what he meant by this, as I clench the piece that Frank sold me. I keep monitoring the security cameras. There is movement out there.

Panthers are naturally solitary. I should not have brought the garage doors to one place. They should have remained in situ, and alone. I keep my eyes on the CCTV. It is totally dark now. The hairs on my arm are standing on end, like lightning is about to strike. The burnished Löwenmensch is now almost too hot to bear. My grip is locked on it. I am unable to let go. Perhaps I've absorbed something from it? The screen flickers. I can no longer make out a human form at the gate. I only see cat eyes flaring bright from the trees. Nine pairs now.

FIREWORK

The crowd gathers in the dismal halflight and drizzle on the tainted patch of meadow left between the ancient concrete and macadam. There will be the tradition of a firework by the dirt river this evening in the muddy zone that no one dares to try to build on. Colour is only barely visible. It's Vember and the grey controller knob has been turned up to maximum. Mostly drowned out by water in various forms some stunted murmurs the only sound of life from those huddled. The night floods in. Leaving just some browns and greens smudged in the drear. Closer inspection revealing these as the leaky reality of the population's woolly damp attempts at protection. Worn ineffectual against the creeping chill. In this old-old park some of the rust of earth almost red still emerges from the decaying leaves that surround the base of these barren trees made of shadows. Soon all the colour will be gone. He must leave before the display. The spectators wait almost expectant. As the rain comes in harder it mutes them still further.

He is already on the road. Out-out over the thousand year old bridge and into the low part of the brick-brick town with the saint's name that is prone to receive the breached waters into its cellars and lower floors. A crumble of terraced buildings line the road as it curves up the last hill. The one that leads towards what was probably called a torway. He walks with purpose up as he traces back the single tramline groove that cuts into the old road from near the river and runs and runs up to way beyond the town's boundary. All the way to the last of the splitting sheds it is said.

About the size of a human head. It is metallic and perfectly square on its visible sides. Annually this blank mirrored box is set on its way through the miasmatic murk. It trundles alone along its metallic notch rumbling and rocking gently as it progresses at a brisk walking pace following the iron slot to the town.

When it passes him he turns back and watches it bobbling away as it disappears into the night. It gently rocks as it descends down through the dilapidated brick-brick of once were factories-churches-schools-pubs and houses. The box shuffles relentless onwards towards the waiting people. Before beginning its journey back it will only rest for a few moments to discharge its silent three second blue-green aurora. The firework that somehow feeds those waiting. Somehow kills them. For this brief display of poison light the sullen always assemble there at this time of year.

Many thanks to Jamie Delano, Barry Hale, Leah Moore (for her Wircus illustrations), Amber Linell, John Higgs, Alan Moore, Geraldine Ryan, Robin Jennings, Daisy Campbell (and all the Horkosians, particularly Michele Olley), to Shardcore for providing a cover for this book to shelter in. And not least to Slim Smith, for his design skills, and internal artwork.